PRAISE FOR ROPE BURN

"If you've been around the great Kirk Sheppard, and you've been around this business, you understand that when it comes to professional wrestling, Kirk just gets it. This book proves that."

— "MACHINE GUN" KARL ANDERSON,
WRESTLING SUPERSTAR

"Kirk Sheppard understands the world of indie wrestling better than anyone."

— BIG MAMA, NWA WOMEN'S WORLD
TELEVISION CHAMPION

Rope Burn

Kirk Sheppard

For Roger, Chad, Jordan, Tasia, and all the boys

Some passions leave marks that never fade.

"This business will never love you back the way you love it."

— JIM ROSS, GOOD OL' JR

ONE

"I guess we'll have to go in another direction."

Stan Weizenschmidt and I stared at our biggest star, Kole the Krusher, with his head cracked open on the cement floor, blood pooling beneath his long blond hair.

We both should have been more rattled by it.

But I had seen worse. Stan had caused worse.

They didn't call him "The Man" in his heyday just for his technical skill—the old-timers still whispered about opponents who never quite wrestled the same after facing him.

Despite the situation with Kole, Stan was calm. Already thinking ahead. He had no choice because in our world the show always goes on.

And he knew I'd help him figure it out.

***

The sickly-sweet smell of spilled beer and popcorn hung in the air of the Elmwood Armory. Three hundred and forty-seven paid to attend WrestleBlast, our biggest show of the year. It was a great house for us, and even more impressive given the snowy conditions outside.

They were there to see Kole, our golden boy, the one Stan had been building the promotion around for the past year.

I watched Kole's accident from my post at the curtain—that thin black barrier separating the fantasy from the chaos backstage—where I stood clipboard in hand, my forty-two-year-old knees already aching from a day on my feet, running back and forth checking on everything—from the PA system to supervising the setup of the ring.

Before Kole had gone out through the curtain, I'd found him in the makeshift locker room, hunched on a bench, staring at his wrestling boots. His eyes looked glassy and unfocused.

"Be ready," I'd called out.

He blinked slowly, raised his head. "Yeah. Yeah, I'm good." His voice was more sluggish than usual. Kole had never been the sharpest, but something was off tonight.

"You sure? You don't look so hot."

"Just tired." He fumbled with his laces, missing the eyelet twice. "Didn't sleep."

Hungover, probably. Kole had been partying hard lately, enjoying the perks of being the top guy in our little corner of the wrestling world.

Five minutes later, Stan appeared beside me, white hair wild, face already flushed with frustration. "His music's been playing for thirty seconds! Where the hell is he?"

"Right here, boss." Kole stood, swaying slightly before finding his balance. He had a million-dollar smile, which had the female fans screaming every Friday night. "Ready to tear the house down."

I caught Stan's sleeve. "He doesn't look right."

Stan yanked his arm free. "He's fine, Luke."

But as Kole's entrance music faded and the bell rang, it was immediately clear that something was wrong.

The match got off to a bad start. Kole's timing was off, and his movements were listless. "Bad" Brad, his opponent, noticed right away, adjusting the pace, calling spots more obviously than usual.

Most of the time, no one could tell when wrestlers were talking to each other in the ring. But tonight, with Kole not at one hundred percent, Brad had to repeat himself. He was yelling at the referee for help in communicating and it wasn't working.

But the crowd didn't seem to care—they were happy to see their hero.

Then it happened. Kole hit the ropes at the wrong angle, too fast, off-balance. Brad charged forward for the spot—a shoulder check designed to send Kole over the top rope into a controlled fall. It was a move they'd done a dozen times before. But Kole didn't grab the rope on his way out of the ring to protect himself. The crack of his head hitting concrete carried over the crowd noise.

I hurried down to ringside. Stan and I, along with the referee, huddled around Kole, not entirely sure what to do. The young security guards, all trainees at Stan's wrestling school, whispered urgently. They waved off any fans that got too close. God forbid we call an ambulance—it would "ruin the show." What Stan really meant was that it would draw the wrong kind of attention. Police, state athletic commissions, insurance adjusters... none of them were welcome in our world.

We sent one of the trainees to grab the stretcher that we'd used earlier for an angle and we gently placed Kole on it and carried him to the locker room.

"Clean up that blood," Stan said, jabbing a finger at a scrawny white kid who probably spent his last paycheck on protein powder and fake tan. The kid didn't hesitate. You didn't question the promoter, not if you had dreams of stepping into that ring one day.

I flagged him down before he scurried off. "The mop is under the ring. Buckets behind the locker room door. Make sure you scrub the cracks in the floor or Stan'll have your head next."

Kole was being carried backstage, limbs dangling like a mannequin. My stomach churned. For three years I'd watched him work his way up from opening matches to main events. Now, he was broken.

"So, now what?" I said, stepping to Stan's side.

His eyes were fixed on the ring, the overhead lights catching the edge of his glasses. "It'll be fine," he said almost to himself.

"He's not fine." I pointed at the trail of blood.

Stan's jaw tightened. For the first time tonight, he looked irritated. "I said, we'll figure it out."

He turned toward the locker room wall where the rundown for the night's matches was fixed with athletic tape. Names were handwritten in black Sharpie, with a number indicating how long their match should go, and the initial of whichever referee was assigned to the pre-determined contest.

Stan's finger traced over "WrestleBlast" on top of the card. He traced Kole's name. The centerpiece, the golden boy, was now done—maybe for good.

Stan's lips pressed into a thin line, and he walked off without a word. Around me, the boys whispered in tight groups, casting uneasy glances at each other.

***

Five minutes after Kole fell out of the ring on his head, the referees still huddled around him in the back, our makeshift medical team doing what little they could. One of our regular fans, who happened to be a chiropractor, used the flashlight from his iPhone to look at Kole's eyes, asked him to count backward from ten, and pronounced him "probably not dying."

Despite the abrupt ending to the match, the crowd was still here, a little confused but also waiting for news about their hero. Someone needed to send them home happy—or at least satisfied.

"I guess I'm closing the show," Stan said, straightening his tie. This situation called for exactly what Stan did best—working a crowd, controlling a narrative, turning disaster into opportunity.

As his entrance music began, I marveled at the transformation from grumpy old promoter to charismatic star. Whatever his flaws were behind the scenes—and there were many—Stan Weizenschmidt knew how to work a crowd.

I tensed as Stan began building to his big announcement.

"Ladies and gentlemen," his voice booming through the PA system, "what you witnessed tonight was just the beginning! 'Bad' Brad Davis and your champion, Kole the Krusher, have unfinished business! And at next month's big event right here in the Elmwood Armory, they will settle it once and for all... INSIDE A STEEL CAGE!"

The crowd erupted, exactly as Stan knew they would. But I froze in disbelief. A cage match? With Kole still leaking from his head? He hadn't even regained consciousness fully, and Stan was already booking him for our most dangerous stipulation match.

Stan continued working the mic, promising the most brutal, high-stakes battle in our promotion's history. The audience ate it up, their earlier concern for Kole's wellbeing forgotten in the excitement of the spectacle to come.

As the crowd filed out, many stopped to shake hands and take selfies with the wrestlers who were strategically positioned by the merchandise table. They were expressing both concern for Kole and excitement for the cage match. Stan stood at the door, selling tickets for the next event. He was unbothered by the fact that he had just committed an injured man to a match he might never be medically cleared for.

The show must go on.

Two

The show had been going well until the main event.

We'd opened with a tag team match. Double Trouble against the Nightmare Express. Double Trouble were the Tucker twins, who worked their synchronized magic to get the crowd energized. Tyler and Travis, identical in their neon green tights, had the audience eating out of their hands as they hit their finishing move—the "Double Down," simultaneous superkicks from opposite sides. The crowd erupted as the referee counted one, two, three.

"Perfect timing," I noted, checking my watch. The match had gone eight minutes—right on schedule.

As Double Trouble celebrated, I signaled to Chuck for the next entrance music. The menacing guitar riffs of "The Blade" Thomas Sharp filled the venue, and the audience's cheers quickly turned to boos.

Sharp emerged from behind the curtain, his black mask covering the upper half of his face, leather trench coat billowing behind him. A mid-forties plumber by day, he committed to his character with remarkable intensity, stalking to the ring as he glared at audience members who dared to make eye contact.

"Who's he working tonight?" Mike asked, his arm wrapped in medical tape. He wasn't scheduled to wrestle until later, giving him time to work through the stiffness in his shoulder.

"A new guy named Eddie Evans," I replied. "I don't know him, but The Blade requested him specifically. Says he saw him on a show in Chicago and liked his work."

The match unfolded as a classic babyface versus heel encounter, building to its inevitable conclusion—Eddie mounting a valiant comeback before Thomas caught him in his "Razor Blade" finisher.

Next came Amber "Lady Liberty" Justice, our only regular female performer—a Black woman in a sport that didn't always make room for one, working a patriotic gimmick in front of a mostly white crowd in Indiana. The crowd genuinely loved her.

Her opponent was "Amazing" Leslie Morgan, a woman we'd booked on Amber's recommendation. Together, they put on arguably the most technically sound match of the night. When Amber secured the victory with her "Liberty Bell" submission, Stan nodded approvingly.

"Crowd stayed with it," he noted with satisfaction. "Might be worth bringing Leslie back next month."

"If we can afford her," I reminded him. Stan waved off the concern.

The next match featured another new talent that Stan was evaluating. "Bulldozer" Bobby Weston, along with his manager Professor Malcolm Pierce, were looking for an opportunity. Their opponent was Stewart Paul—six-foot-six, pushing four hundred pounds, a security guard at the local high school who'd been working our shows for years as "The Starmaker." He moved better than a man his size had any right to. For the finish, Pierce's interference backfired spectacularly, and Stew capitalized with a quick roll-up to secure the upset. The crowd loved it.

I wasn't impressed with the new guys, but Stew made them look better than they were.

And then there was the semi-main event. Mike "The Bruiser" Alvarez and Jim "The Hammer" Tanner's match delivered exactly what we needed—a clinic in old-school wrestling that had the audience fully invested. The pairing was complementary: Mike, with his twenty years in the business including stints in Japan and Mexico, against Jim, the technical purist who'd trained at that legendary camp in Minneapolis, where technique was religion.

Jim had come closer than most to making it to the big time, with those television appearances on syndicated shows that almost led to something bigger. Outside the ring, his life mirrored his wrestling—methodical and disciplined. His building inspector job provided stability that wrestling couldn't, especially after his wife Maggie's cancer took her seven years ago, leaving him to raise their son alone. Jim's dinners with his son were the one commitment that superseded wrestling.

Twelve minutes in, they built to a classic finish—Jim overcoming Mike's assault on his leg to hit the "Hammer Time" combo, a spinebuster followed by a top-rope elbow drop. The three-count was academic at that point. The crowd rose to their feet.

"Now, that's wrestling," Stan said as they made their way back through the curtain. "Not that shit on TV these days."

Finally, it was time for the main event. Kole was defending his championship against "Bad" Brad Davis. Brad was one of our most reliable workers—not flashy, but technically sound and safe in the ring. The best opponent for a big show like this. We'd been building this program with him and Kole for nearly two months.

It was supposed to be a hell of a main event.

THREE

AFTER MOST OF the fans had filed out, I found Stan in the converted storage closet he used as an office. He was hunched over a stack of papers, calculator in hand, muttering numbers under his breath.

"Kole should go to a hospital," I said, leaning against the doorframe. "Probably a concussion. Maybe worse."

Stan didn't look up. "We sold a hundred tickets for next month's show." He punched numbers into the calculator.

"I don't know if he'll be okay by then."

"Says who?"

"Says common sense, Stan. He couldn't remember his own name ten minutes ago."

Stan finally looked up, reading glasses perched on the end of his nose. "Did he actually say that, or are you being dramatic?"

"When I asked if he knew where he was, he said 'Tuesday.'"

Stan frowned. "It's Friday."

"Exactly."

He removed his glasses, pinching the bridge of his nose. We

could hear the crew breaking down the ring, the metallic clang of steel pipes being stacked on the truck.

"So what do you suggest?" Stan asked, an edge to his voice.

"We'll have to find another opponent for Brad."

"Who?" Stan threw his hands up. "We announced Kole defending his title—and I made this cage match seem like a major deal."

The cage hadn't been part of the plan, but then again, Stan sometimes didn't share his creative vision with me. Regardless, now that he had announced it, we had to deliver.

But we had a concussed champion who could barely stand.

Jim poked his head in, still in his ring gear, a sheen of sweat glistening on his forehead.

"I'm taking Kole to the ER," he said.

"Just don't tell them he did it wrestling. Insurance won't pay. And I don't need anybody from the commission nosing around," Stan said.

Jim ignored him. "What are we gonna do about the cage next month?"

Stan looked up sharply. "Why does everyone assume that he—"

"Because his brains are scrambled," Jim cut in, voice matter-of-fact. "And not just because he fell out of the ring tonight."

"I'll wait for him to be medically cleared before I book him," Stan said.

"Make him bring a note from his doctor." Jim crossed his arms. "Because he'll tell you he's okay, whether it's true or not."

Stan waved a hand. "We'll figure something out."

Jim nodded, satisfied for now, and ducked back out.

Stan looked at me. "I don't have time for this."

Neither did I. But it would keep me up all night.

Four

A server crash alert hit my phone at 3:17 AM a week later.

My eyes burned as I squinted at the notification: PRIORITY ALERT: CUSTOMER PORTAL DOWN.

"Shit," I muttered, rolling out of bed. Some of my coworkers would sleep through these middle-of-the-night alerts, dealing with them at 9 AM when they got into the office. But I didn't have that luxury. I needed my job too much, especially with my overdue performance review looming.

Ten minutes later, unshowered but caffeinated, I sat at my kitchen table tracing the issue through our system. Someone had pushed through an untested update, crashing the portal.

Twenty minutes of debugging and a few lines of code fixed the issue. It was nothing complicated, but it did require careful attention to detail.

By 4:45 AM, I sent an all-clear email, subtly highlighting that I'd corrected someone's mistake.

I didn't go back to sleep.

I badged in at 6:27 AM to Silvertech Solutions, which was housed in a sleek seven-floor glass-and-steel office building.

Despite it being Martin Luther King, Jr. Day, we were expected to work. The security guard gave me a nod as I passed the untouched ping-pong table, the already-depleted vending machine, and the motivational posters with their stock photos of diverse people finding apparent fulfillment in database management. I liked the early mornings; the empty, quiet office gave me three uninterrupted hours before the morning stand-up would fill the space with chatter and office politics.

My desk was in the middle of the open-plan floor. My role was not prestigious enough for a private office or even a window. On my desk: two company-issued monitors, a keyboard, and a cactus that survived three years of neglect. There were no photos or artifacts from my other world; I kept my wrestling life separate from this place, though a few coworkers had found out about my "hobby" and asked awkward questions.

Questions like "isn't that shit fake?"

I dove into my assignments, coding and problem solving and responding to emails about coding and problem solving. The technical work came easily—I'd always understood systems, how pieces fit together. It was the corporate ecosystem I struggled with: the politics, the networking, the unwritten rules of advancement.

By 9:15, Eric had summoned me to his glass-walled office.

"Hey Luke, thanks for fixing that issue last night."

"Sure thing," I said.

My phone buzzed.

> Warehouse 5:30 today. New guys
> signing up to train.

I typed back:

> Will try. Deadline crunch.

Stan replied instantly:

I need you.

Eric was waiting for me to look up. "I'll cut right to the chase. The senior position requires someone fully committed," Eric said. "Your technical skills are strong, but your focus seems... elsewhere."

"No, I'm good. I can handle it."

"We'll see. I need you to finish the Richardson project today. OK?"

"Of course."

I finished the Richardson implementation with twenty minutes to spare.

I had just enough time to heat up the sad frozen dinner I'd stashed in the break room before heading to the warehouse. My phone buzzed again with a calendar reminder.

JANUARY 20th. FIRST DAY AT SWP.

The microwave dinged, and I stared at the steaming plastic tray of what allegedly was chicken Alfredo. Fifteen years ago today, I'd first walked into Stan Weizenschmidt's world, and I still couldn't decide if it had been the best day of my life or the worst.

I was twenty-eight, with a fresh computer science degree and one year of professional experience maintaining websites for businesses that couldn't afford real tech teams.

The flyer had caught my eye outside a convenience store:

"PROFESSIONAL WRESTLING—LIVE!" splashed across the top in garish red letters. Below that, a low-resolution photo of a muscular man in black trunks holding a championship belt overhead. The rest of the design was a crime against graphic design—at least three mismatched fonts, clip art, and a color scheme that made my eyes hurt.

And at the top: "Stan Weizenschmidt Promotions."

I'd grown up watching Stan "The Man" Weizenschmidt on TV, at the end of the days when territories still existed, and wrestling still felt magical. My mother used to complain about "that fake garbage," while my father and I would watch it together.

My heart would race when the opening theme music started. The characters, the feuds, the simple morality plays—good versus evil with bodyslams and piledrivers. Other kids outgrew their wrestling phase. I never did.

I kept the flyer folded in my back pocket all week, occasionally taking it out to look at the cartoonish graphics and the date of the upcoming show. The website listed at the bottom seemed like it could use help from someone who knew what they were doing.

I sat at my computer, clicking through the abysmal design. Broken links. Outdated information. A "News" section that hadn't been updated in eighteen months. The whole thing looked like it had been built in 1998 and abandoned shortly after.

My mind raced with potential improvements, designs that could transform the digital wasteland into something professional. This wasn't just about building my portfolio anymore.

When I finally got the courage to drive to the dingy warehouse, I could hear the unmistakable sound of bodies hitting canvas. I hesitated. I was just a web designer with a proposal and a childhood obsession. I had no business being there.

Despite all that, I stepped inside.

The warehouse was smaller than it looked from outside. In the center was a wrestling ring that had seen better days. A single row of folding chairs lined one wall. Exposed pipes leaked from the ceiling, with a collection of strategically placed buckets underneath. A handful of men in various states of athletic wear were running drills under the watchful eye of an older man whose white hair stood out starkly against his deeply tanned skin.

Stan Weizenschmidt. Older than he was last time I saw him on TV, but unmistakable.

"Can I help you?"

The voice came from my right—a bored-looking woman behind a folding table. Her bleached blonde hair was pulled back in a messy ponytail, a half-eaten sandwich sat beside her outdated computer.

"I, uh—" I fumbled for words, feeling foolish. "I saw your flyer. And your website. I'm a web designer, actually, and I thought maybe I could offer my services."

"You want to work for us?"

"I mean, I could update your site. Make it more professional. More user-friendly." I was rambling now. "I just thought—"

"Who's this, Shari?"

Stan had noticed me and was making his way over, leaving his trainees to continue their drills.

"Says he's a web designer," she replied with a smirk. "Wants to fix our website." She emphasized the word *fix* as if the very concept was amusing.

Stan looked me up and down, the way you'd size up a piece of equipment to see if it was worth keeping. I knew what he saw: average height, average build, nothing remarkable. Not wrestler material.

"You a fan?" he asked.

"Yes, sir." The *sir* slipped out automatically. "I watched you all through the eighties. The program with Koslov was incredible."

Something flickered in Stan's eyes—validation, perhaps, from being recognized. At having his glory days remembered.

"The website, huh? What's wrong with it?"

"It's—" I stopped myself from saying *terrible.* "It could be more effective. Your show schedule is hard to find, there's no way to buy tickets online, and the loading time is pretty slow."

Stan's expression didn't change. "So, what would you charge? And don't say it's expensive, because we're not exactly WWE over here."

The question was abrupt, all business.

"I, uh—I could do a basic redesign for free. If you want something more complex, we could work something out." Then I added: "Maybe you could just comp me tickets to your shows?"

Stan's eyes narrowed, calculating something. "You'd work for tickets?"

FIVE

"Sign here, initial here, and here… and sign here." My voice was mechanical. I'd explained the training school contract so many times I could do it in my sleep.

Stan had started his wrestling academy as both a feeder system for SWP and as a way to make more money. New students rarely asked questions, but when they did, those questions told me everything. The guys who asked how binding the contract was? Already halfway to quitting before their first bump.

I wasn't kind about it. "Thinking about quitting already? Maybe we save time and rip this up now." They'd squirm, but no one ever took me up on the offer. But eventually, most of them quietly quit showing up.

Joey Davis was another dreamer handing over his savings to chase a fantasy. He signed his name on the training contract like it was a sacred document.

He was just over six feet tall with short blond hair. Clean-cut and handsome, the kind of guy that would appeal to female fans without alienating their boyfriends. He wore a simple gray t-shirt that had seen better days and his gym shorts hung loose on his wiry frame.

He was too skinny to make it, I thought. That was the standard—too skinny or too fat, too soft or too lazy. He handed over his cash quickly, almost too quickly, like he feared I might change my mind about letting him enroll.

"Thanks," he said, polite and soft-spoken. He hovered by the desk a moment, as if unsure whether to say something else, before heading to the ring room.

Trent Howard walked in five minutes after Joey, a towering 6'3" figure that commanded immediate attention. His thick black hair, striking large eyes, and muscular physique were what wrestling promoters dream about. His fitted button-up strained against his chest and shoulders. He handed me his cash but held on just long enough to make me tug it from his fingers.

I could already tell Trent would be one of *those* guys.

"So," he smirked. "When do I get my first title shot?"

"You're funny," I said.

Trent chuckled. He gestured toward the ring room. "Guess I'll head in and get started."

"Guess you will," I said as he strolled past.

<hr>

Joey was already sitting on a chair near the edge of the ring. His hands were clasped in front of him, like he wasn't sure what to do with them.

Trent stood by the ring like he owned it.

Joey gave him a polite nod. Trent ignored him.

"Alright, ladies!" Stan's voice boomed through the warehouse door as he finally made his entrance. "Let's see what we're working with today."

Joey snapped to attention, while Trent stood relaxed. Stan

surveyed them both with the practiced eye of someone who'd evaluated physical potential for decades. His gaze lingered on Trent, interest flickering across his face before turning to Joey with considerably less enthusiasm.

"Your first day is about the fundamentals," Stan announced, climbing into the ring. "Most important thing in wrestling isn't the flashy moves. It's learning how to fall without breaking your neck."

He demonstrated a basic back bump, body flat against the canvas, arms at forty-five-degree angles, his chin tucked to his chest. Even at sixty-three years old, there was something impressive about Stan's movement in the ring.

"Like this," Stan said, falling backwards again, slapping the mat with both palms as he landed. "Distribute the impact. Tuck your head. You're gonna do this thousands of times. If you stick around."

Joey nodded earnestly. Trent looked bored.

"You," Stan pointed at Joey. "You're up."

Joey stepped forward, mimicking Stan's position. He went down awkwardly, body tense, impact uneven. He winced as his elbow took too much weight.

"Again," Stan ordered, not unkindly. "Relax this time. You're too stiff."

They spent thirty minutes on back bumps before moving to forward rolls. Joey improved with each attempt, his body gradually adapting to unfamiliar movements. Trent, unsurprisingly, picked things up faster, his natural athleticism compensating for inexperience.

By the time they moved to running the ropes, both recruits showed signs of wear. Joey's elbows were red from repeated contact with the mat, while Trent had worked up a sweat that darkened his shirt.

"This," Stan said, bouncing off the ropes with practiced ease, "is where the real pain is."

He demonstrated proper technique, his back hitting the middle rope while his arm hooked over the top one for safety. "Your back hits here. Not your arm, not your neck. Your back."

Joey went first, approaching the ropes with the same cautious determination he'd shown with bumps. He threw himself forward, but when he hit the ropes, his positioning was wrong. The top rope caught right under his arm.

He let out a sharp breath, stumbling forward instead of rebounding cleanly. The red welt forming under his arm didn't look like much yet, but by tomorrow it would be an angry purple bruise.

"Back in," Stan ordered. "You'll get it eventually or you won't."

For the next forty-five minutes, they walked—then ran—the ropes. Joey improved gradually, his technique refining with each painful attempt. Trent didn't fare much better. Even natural talent couldn't prevent the ropes from exacting their toll.

As Stan wrapped up their first session, I noticed Trent gingerly holding his arms away from his body, the fresh rope burns too tender to touch. Joey had similar marks but didn't let on that he was in pain.

"You're gonna be sore. Tomorrow will be rough. But," I said, "it's the next day when you really feel the burn."

Six

My phone lay on the foldout table, its vibration barely audible over the thuds of bodies hitting the mat.

TWO MISSED CALLS – ERIC (WORK).

Two weeks into training, and the new guys were making progress. Across the ring, Mike was running Joey through basic chain wrestling while Jim worked with some of the more experienced trainees in the corner. Trent was running late again, something that was becoming a pattern.

Another buzz. NEW EMAIL – URGENT: SERVER ISSUES.

"Jesus Christ." I was trying to update the flyer for Friday night's show, but this couldn't wait. I connected to Silvertech's servers through the VPN.

Luke,
   I don't know where you are, but we have an issue with the

login portal. If you could take two minutes to look at the ticket, that'd be great.

Eric

I clenched my jaw. The subtext was clear. I was letting the team down. Again.

My eyes darted back to the ring. Joey was listening intently as Mike demonstrated an arm drag.

Back to my laptop, I typed furiously while keeping one eye on the half-finished graphics on the other half of my screen.

"Is my marketing material interrupting your day job?"

I hadn't heard Stan approach. He stood behind me, his voice both full of annoyance and resignation.

"Server emergency," I explained, not looking up. "Five minutes, tops."

"Just make sure those flyers are done today. We need to get them to the print shop by tomorrow."

"Will do."

The door swung open, and Trent sauntered in nearly thirty minutes late, gym bag slung casually over his shoulder.

"Nice of you to join us," Stan called out, his tone lighter than I expected.

Trent flashed a grin. "Traffic."

Mike paused his session with Joey, barely disguising his irritation. "Get warmed up," he said flatly.

I turned back to my computer, sent a quick fix to Eric, and pulled the flyer back up.

***

Fifteen years ago—three weeks into my tenure as official web designer for SWP—I sat in the half-filled Elmwood Armory watching mediocre matches. There were issues with the sound system that made the entrance music sound like it came through a broken drive-thru speaker. The crowd was small. Stan was frustrated.

"Hey, Stan," I said. "So . . . you know how I said we could start selling tickets on the web site?"

"Yeah?"

"There's seventy-one pre-sold tickets for next week's show."

"Through the website? That can't be right."

"I can show you." I pulled up the report on my laptop.

"Huh," he said. "Kid, you might be a fucking genius."

Stan's acknowledgment sent a wave of electricity through me. Those three weeks of late nights, coding the site, learning e-commerce integration, setting up payment processing. Hours stolen from sleep after my regular job duties were handled.

Worth it.

Later, as I was driving home, my phone rang. Stan's name was on the display. I answered immediately, turning down the radio.

"Luke? You home yet?" Stan's voice riding the post-show adrenaline I was learning was typical for him.

"Almost. What's up?"

"Been thinking about what you said. About the online merch store. The—what'd you call it?"

"Print on demand," I supplied. "So, we don't have to carry inventory or—"

"Yeah, yeah, that's it." Stan cut me off, too excited to let me finish. "We should do it. Set it up. You can handle that, right? Put those computer skills to work?"

I pulled into my apartment complex but didn't get out. "Sure, I can set that up. Might take a week or two to get the designs ready and—"

"Perfect. I knew you'd figure it out. And that thing you said about the mailing list, collecting emails at shows. We should do that too. Build the—whatcha call it?"

"The audience database," I said, unable to keep the smile off my face.

"That's it! The database." Stan was full-on excited, ideas tumbling out faster than he could articulate. "Send them updates, upcoming shows, pictures of the boys. Get them invested in the stories. Goddamn brilliant, Luke."

I sat in my car. Stan was talking about *my* ideas. Not just implementing them but embracing them.

"We'll talk about all of it Monday," Stan continued. "Come by the warehouse around 5? Bring your computer. And those things for the email signups."

"Sure," I agreed.

"You're saving my ass here, Luke. This online stuff is the future. And you're the first guy who's done it right."

I checked my watch. Nine hours until brunch with Mom and Dad. I should sleep, but my mind raced with ideas for the merch store, email templates, website refinements. I'd spend the weekend on it.

Anything to make Stan happy.

Seven

The date on my watch confirmed what I'd been trying to ignore all day: March 5th. My birthday.

My phone buzzed for the third time in ten minutes. I knew without looking who it was. I slipped the phone from my pocket just enough to see Mom's name on the screen. Forty-three years old and I was still dodging my mother's calls like a teenager. Appropriate, since her messages always made me feel about sixteen again.

The vibration stopped abruptly as the call went to voicemail.

Mike was sitting on the ring apron. "Everything okay?" he asked, wrapping athletic tape around his wrists.

"Fine. Just my mother." I didn't need to listen to the voicemail to know what she'd say: her annual reminder of opportunities missed and expectations unmet, with "happy birthday" added as an afterthought.

"Hey, isn't today your—"

"Yep." I cut Mike off. "No big deal."

"Well, happy birthday, man."

"Thanks." I was already focusing on the lineup for Friday's show.

Stan didn't have patience for birthdays unless someone was buying a package of tickets to our show. He didn't see value in sentimentality, not if it wasn't monetized. That was fine with me; I hadn't liked celebrating since my father died ten years ago this week.

Stan surprised me by attending the funeral. He'd shown up with Shari, his girlfriend at the time, wearing an actual suit instead of his usual track pants and polo shirt. Maybe Shari had made him come, or maybe he just knew it was the right thing to do. Either way, it was one of the few times I'd seen real compassion from "The Man."

He shook my hand, gave me half a hug, and we never mentioned it again.

The warehouse was alive with slamming bodies and shouts of "Again!" as trainees worked through evening drills. There were eight or nine guys running the ropes, hitting bags, and practicing chain wrestling. Joey was there early, stretching on the mats as always. Jim was there to work with the younger students, something he did from time to time.

The massive sliding door in the back of the warehouse stood open for the first time in months, admitting sunlight and the tentative warmth of March. After an endless Indiana winter in the stale confines of our humble facility, fresh air felt like a revelation. A few of the guys dragged mats outside to stretch in the sun, their pale skin almost luminous after months indoors.

"Jesus! You boys need to find a tanning bed," Stan said.

Our training facility occupied a former medical supply distribution center on Elmwood's outskirts. The main room housed the ring at its center, with a smaller room off to the side, full of weight equipment salvaged from three different failed gyms. Exposed ductwork hung from the ceiling, and concrete floors remained permanently stained with mysterious industrial residue.

The walls, originally institutional beige, had been painted deep red and were haphazardly covered with wrestling posters from both Stan's heyday and SWP's most recent shows. There was a championship belt above the door frame, and next to the door were a few inspirational quotes Stan had torn from fitness magazines. What the warehouse lacked in aesthetics, it made up for in affordability.

Years ago, one of the trainees—a guy with a construction shoot job—framed an area that served as Stan's office. There was a door, which he closed only when he didn't want to be bothered. Just outside the office was the folding table that functioned as my desk. It's where I kept the promotion running with a giant calendar listing who was booked on which show. It was also where I sat with my laptop—where I updated the website, designed the show graphics, and tracked the finances. Stan kept me in the dark about money most of the time; he only gave me the financial data to enter in Quickbooks every quarter or so. Or whenever he remembered.

Training started and Stan paced the edge of the ring, barking instructions at trainees fumbling through a basic sequence. "No, no! Back to the headlock. Clean this time!"

"Square your shoulders when you lock up," Jim was on the floor. He was demonstrating the perfect stance to one of the other newer guys. "Stand up straight! Wrestling is built on fundamentals —master them first." He sighed. "These kids today want to skip right to the flashy stuff."

Trent strolled in, gym bag slung over one shoulder. Late again.

"You're just in time," I said, not looking up from my paperwork. "Missed the warmups. Again."

Trent flashed his usual grin. "I'm never late for showtime."

"Trent!" Stan called out. "Get warmed up. You're gonna put together a basic match with Joey tonight."

Hearing his name, Joey looked over from the ring where he was waiting his turn for the next drill.

"Joey?" Trent glanced toward Stan, clearly hoping for reassignment. "Figured you'd want me with someone more... established."

Stan shook his head. "Get in there."

Joey's hands tightened into fists, but he said nothing as Trent climbed into the ring, taking his time. The other trainees jumped out onto the floor, ready to watch.

"All right, kid," Trent said, loud enough for everyone to hear. "Try to keep up."

They locked up in the middle of the ring. Joey moved fast, slipping behind Trent and locking in a waistlock, but Trent easily reversed it, shoving Joey forward and slapping him on the back of the head.

"Lighten up," Stan called from ringside.

Joey spun around, face tight, and locked up with Trent again. This time, Joey got the upper hand, rolling Trent into a quick headlock takedown. Trent kicked out easily, kipping up to his feet, grinning like he'd planned it all along.

"That all you got, kid?"

Joey didn't answer.

They went through a short chain sequence, Joey listening to Trent's whispered instructions. Trent called for an Irish whip, but instead of running into the ropes, he jumped out of the ring to catch his breath.

"What the fuck was that?" Stan demanded.

Trent smirked. "Just pacing myself, boss."

"Cardio not your thing?" I asked.

Joey stood in the center of the ring, breathing hard but ready. Trent waved him off.

"We good?" Trent asked Stan. "I got the gist."

"No," Stan said firmly. "I said I wanted to see a basic match. You didn't even run a single spot."

Trent got back in the ring and locked up with Joey again. This time, Joey got him in a wristlock, grinding just enough to make Trent wince. Joey's eyes flicked toward Stan—checking if he was doing it right—and Stan nodded.

"Good," Stan said, "Keep going."

After two minutes of very basic stuff, Trent rolled Joey up for a pin and counted to three himself.

Stan gave them light critique and was mostly positive. Trent climbed out the ring first, grabbing his water bottle and toweling off like he'd finished a main event. Joey stayed behind, leaning against the ropes, catching his breath.

Once Joey climbed out, he grabbed a broom to sweep the mats. After a few minutes, he paused, leaning on the broom, and looked longingly at the ring.

Stan wandered over, watching Joey with an assessing eye.

"Kid works hard," I said.

"Not star material though," Stan replied, shaking his head. "Not like Trent. That kid will sell tickets."

I said nothing, but when Stan moved away to yell at another trainee, I picked up my pen and made a note in the margin of the training log.

Joey = star?

Eight

"Kid, you got your gear?" Stan asked him, a couple of weeks later.

"Yessir," Joey said.

"Good. You're having your first match tonight."

The match was just filler. Fourth on the card, a quick five-minute bout to give the crowd a breather before the featured women's match, just prior to intermission. Nobody expected much from it. We hadn't even told Joey until that afternoon. That was Stan's usual way of doing things—don't give them too much time to be nervous, but also minimize the moment so they don't get an ego.

And make them lose. Always make them lose their first one.

I stood backstage, arms crossed, watching Joey prepare. He was wrestling "The Bruiser," Mike's in-ring moniker. As one of our veteran heels, Mike wasn't flashy, but he was reliable. And he was big enough to look threatening, loud enough to get heat, and smart enough to make a kid like Joey's first match a success.

"You listening?" Mike barked in the locker room, his voice booming. Joey nodded, face pale but focused.

"First, we'll give you a little shine," Mike said, pacing. "Let the crowd see what you've got. Then I'm taking over. The heat's on me—you sell it like I'm killing you out there. When it's time for the comeback, don't rush. Make 'em want it. And then I'll go over. Smooth. Easy."

"Yes, sir."

The bell rang, and Mike went to work. He shoved Joey into the corner and flexed for the crowd, shouting, "Is this all you've got?!" The boos rolled in and Mike soaked them up, turning to yell at a fan in the second row. Joey watched, waiting for his moment.

Mike charged forward with a clothesline, but Joey ducked, hitting the ropes and coming back with a dropkick that sent Mike stumbling. Joey scrambled to his feet, hit the ropes again, and connected with another dropkick that sent Mike to the floor. The crowd cheered as Mike made a show of his frustration.

When he got back in the ring, Mike cut him off quickly—one big boot to the chest, and Joey was flat on his back. That was it for the shine.

Next was the heat, the part where the bad guy takes control. Mike dragged Joey to his feet, muttering just loud enough for him to hear. "Stay loose. Let 'em feel it." He whipped Joey into the turnbuckle, then charged in for a running splash. Joey collapsed to the mat, clutching his ribs, face twisted in pain.

"Good," Mike growled, grabbing Joey by the hair and hauling him to the center of the ring. "Let's take it nice and slow."

He locked Joey into a chinlock, wrenching his head back and grinning at the crowd, who responded with louder boos. Joey flailed, clawing at Mike's arms, reaching desperately for the ropes. His fingers brushed the bottom one, and the crowd started clapping again, urging him on. A kid in the front row stood up and shouted, "Come on, Joey!"

Mike yanked him back to the center of the ring. More boos. Louder this time.

"Time for the comeback," Mike whispered as he hauled Joey up again. "Make it count."

Joey reversed an Irish whip, sending Mike into the ropes, and caught him with a flying forearm on the rebound. Mike staggered but didn't fall. Joey hit him with another forearm, then a dropkick that finally sent the big man crashing into the turnbuckle. The crowd erupted, stomping and clapping as Joey climbed the ropes.

He perched on the second turnbuckle, fists clenched, and leapt off with a flying crossbody. He connected cleanly, and the ref slid into position for the count.

One. Two.

Mike kicked out.

Joey's eyes widened as he scrambled to his feet, glancing toward the ropes. Without slowing down, he went back for more —leaping off the top this time.

But with one swift move, Mike caught him, spun around, and drove him into the mat with a powerslam. The crash echoed through the ring, rattling the ropes. The crowd gasped.

One. Two. Three.

The bell rang, and the ref raised Mike's hand. He celebrated, earning boos from the crowd, while Joey lay on the mat staring at the ceiling. Joey was breathing hard, but as he got to his feet, the crowd gave an unexpectedly loud round of applause.

Mike was waiting for him by the curtain. "Not bad, kid." He shook Joey's hand.

"Thank you, sir," Joey said, beaming like he couldn't believe he'd just had his first match in front of an audience.

As he sat down and started undoing the laces on his boots, Joey's eyes met mine, searching my face for approval. He came over to where I was standing.

"Was that okay?" he asked.

"You listened. Didn't screw it up."

"Thanks." His shoulders relaxed, and he let out a breathless laugh.

"Anyone from your family here to see it?"

"My mom had to work tonight, but hopefully someone filmed it so I can show her later."

"Good work, Joey."

As he walked away, I found myself smiling. Just a little.

Lady Liberty's entrance music—a remixed version of "America the Beautiful" with a pulsing beat—filled the Armory. The crowd, already warm from Joey's debut, came alive as Amber Justice emerged through the curtain. Her ring gear was a stylized red, white, and blue ensemble: wrestling boots adorned with white stars, blue tights with white piping, and a cropped top patterned after the American flag.

"Making her way to the ring," the announcer's voice boomed, "representing truth, justice, and the American way—LADY LIBERTY...AMBER JUSTICE!"

Amber had the crowd wrapped around her finger, high-fiving kids in the front row and pointing to a homemade sign that read "LADY LIBERTY 4 PRESIDENT." Unlike some of the manufactured characters Stan forced on wrestlers, Amber's patriotic gimmick worked because she'd developed it herself, refining it over four years on the indie circuit before joining us.

"Full house tonight," she remarked as she passed me on her way to the ring.

"Two-fifty paid," I confirmed. "Your Instagram post helped."

She flashed a smile and adjusted her championship belt—a women's title Stan had introduced two years ago when he finally saw that women's wrestling was starting to draw money. That decision had been one of his rare moments of adaptability, though he'd resisted until Amber proved herself by consistently getting the loudest reactions on the card.

Her opponent tonight was Vanessa "The Vixen" Torres, a powerhouse from Chicago whom Amber had suggested. The two had history, having trained at Sully's Wrestling Academy in Milwaukee before taking different paths. While Amber built her Lady Liberty persona on the Midwest circuit, Vanessa had spent three years in Japan. Her hard-hitting style contrasted well with Amber's more technical approach.

As Vanessa made her entrance—complete with a Japanese headdress she discarded at ringside—I noticed Stan standing beside me.

"This better be good," he muttered. "I'm paying Torres double what we usually offer."

"Amber says she's worth it," I replied. "Plus, having someone of her caliber makes the women's division stronger."

Stan snorted. "Division? We've got Amber and whoever she brings in. That's not a division; it's a novelty act."

I bit my tongue. We'd had this argument before. Despite the fact that women's wrestling was drawing record audiences for the major promotions, Stan remained convinced it was a passing trend, not worth serious investment.

While she was a draw, I liked having her on the card because Amber's presence changed the energy in the locker room. In a world of testosterone and traditionalism, she'd carved out not just a place for herself but was actively working to expand opportunities for other women. All while consistently delivering some of our best matches.

"Just watch," I said.

The bell rang. Amber and Vanessa worked at a pace and intensity that hooked the crowd immediately. What began as cordial competition escalated as Vanessa unleashed a series of stiff forearms that echoed through the hall. Amber, rather than backing down, fired back with strikes that sent her larger opponent reeling.

As the crowd reacted, I said to Stan, "Told you."

"Still gotta draw to justify the paycheck," he countered.

Trent, who was watching the show through the curtain, had his arms crossed. "First Joey and now this? While I just sit back here doing nothing," he said just loud enough for us to hear.

I turned to read him the riot act, but Stan got there first. "You'll get your spot. That's why you're back here and not out there doing security. I want your debut to be special."

Twelve minutes in, both women were showing the effects of the match. A thin trickle of blood ran from Amber's lower lip where she'd caught an errant knee, and Vanessa was selling her left leg after a well-executed dragon screw leg whip. The crowd was chanting "Liberty! Liberty!" as Amber countered Vanessa's power-bomb attempt into a hurricanrana.

"They're going long," Stan said, checking his watch. "Should've wrapped it up two minutes ago."

As if she heard him, Amber locked Vanessa in her finisher—the "Liberty Bell," a modified STF that targeted the leg she'd been working on while she applied a painful crossface to the upper body. Vanessa fought valiantly but ultimately tapped out to end the contest.

The crowd erupted, jumping to their feet as Lady Liberty retained her championship. Amber helped Vanessa up, and the two embraced in a show of sportsmanship that drew another round of cheers.

"Well," Stan said as they made their way backstage, "that was better than I expected."

Amber's face was flushed as she came through the curtain, belt over her shoulder. "Told you she was good," she said to me, dabbing at her lip with a towel.

"You were both excellent," I agreed. "That sequence where you reversed the German suplex—"

"All her," Amber said, gesturing to Vanessa who was now coming through the curtain. "That's what you get when you bring in someone who's worked the Tokyo Dome."

Vanessa was beaming. "Thanks for the opportunity," she said, extending her hand to Stan. "Would love to come back if you'll have me."

Stan, ever the businessman, didn't commit at first. "We'll talk. Good showing tonight."

As he walked away, Amber rolled her eyes. "That's Stan-speak for 'I'm impressed but don't want to admit it,'" she explained to Vanessa. "He'll call you."

The two women headed for the women's locker room, which was really just a corner of the room we'd draped off with a tarp.

It had taken us three months after Kole's devastating injury to finally resolve the championship situation.

First, we threw our lovable super-heavyweight, Stewie "The Starmaker" Paul, in as a last-minute replacement for the cage match against Brad—a mismatch resulting in twenty minutes of sluggish pacing as the big guy struggled to keep up. Luckily, a run-in by Jim "The Hammer" had redeemed things with the crowd and set up a match between him and Brad last month, which led to tonight's main event ladder match.

"Stan sure did book his way out of that one," Mike observed.

"I just hope the ladder is special enough that people forgive the cage bait-and-switch," I added.

"It'll be great." Mike chuckled. "And the way Stan told the story in that promo he cut—'This championship is so important, we're hanging it high above the ring where only the most deserving competitor can reach it'—you'd think he planned it all along."

"So, how is Kole?"

"I haven't heard from him, but Stan said six more months minimum," I confirmed. "That's if everything goes perfectly. Nerve damage doesn't heal like a broken bone."

Mike let out a low whistle. "Poor kid. Top of the world one minute, career in jeopardy the next."

"That's the business."

We all knew Stan had been holding out hope, refusing to officially vacate after Kole's injury. "He's a fast healer," Stan had insisted. But eventually I convinced him that we needed to move on. We needed a champion.

Jim sat next to his cooler filled with ice water, trunks on, and boots almost laced. His weathered face wore a mask of focus. At forty-four, Jim was our veteran, the guy who'd seen it all, done it all, and somehow kept coming back.

"How's the house?" he asked as he taped his wrists.

"Three hundred and twelve paid," I reported. "Pretty good!"

Jim just nodded. He'd been in this business since I was in college, had put superstars over in arenas ten times this size in his prime on syndicated television. Winning our title wasn't going to be the highlight of his career.

Jim noticed Joey across the room. "Looks like the kid's got something. He listens. That's rare these days."

"He does," I agreed, thinking about how Joey had sold Mike's offense, made the crowd care enough to cheer for a losing performance.

"What's next?" Jim asked, seeming to read my thoughts. "After tonight? Stan got his eye on anyone for my first defense?"

"I don't know."

Jim's hands paused in their taping. "Well, I'll do whatever he needs."

Stan came raging through the curtain. "Can you believe these idiots?" he raged, not directing his question at anyone in particular. "We're out of hot dogs already. And ice! ALREADY! And it's not even intermission! Where did all the fucking ice go?"

He spotted us and changed tracks. "Jim! The ladder's under the ring. You'll need to—"

"I know, Stan," Jim cut in calmly. "We've been over it three times today."

"And I want Trent watching your match closely from backstage. I'm thinking of teaming you two up, veteran and rookie. Could be good chemistry."

Jim raised an eyebrow at this but agreed. "Sure, Stan. Whatever you think is best."

Stan stormed off toward the concession stand, no doubt to continue berating the volunteers who showed up every Friday to work, just to say they were part of SWP. Joey walked over, already in his street clothes, and wished Jim good luck in his match.

"Great match out there, kid," Jim told him. "Keep that up and you'll be in the main event sooner than you think."

Joey's eyes widened. "Thank you, sir. That means a lot."

"Why are you dressed?" I asked.

"I thought you'd need me to do security for the main event?" Joey said.

"No! You had a match. I need you to go out and sign autographs at intermission with the other babyfaces. Put your gear back on."

"Yessir!" He scrambled away.

Jim smiled at me. "Are you ribbing him?"

"Only a little. I do want him to sign autographs. We've got plenty of security tonight. But he doesn't really need to put his gear back on. That was just for fun."

Nine

The Wing Place was packed, as it always was after our shows. The wrestlers had claimed our usual corner—three tables pushed together near the jukebox that perpetually played Skynyrd and Hank Jr. while fans milled around, some seeking autographs while others just enjoyed their meals while talking about the show they'd just seen.

Jim was nursing a beer. While the title belt would normally be in his gear bag, at Stan's insistence it was now resting on the table beside a plate of half-eaten wings. "The fans will want their picture with you, it'll go on social media, and we'll get more buzz," he explained, as if he had ever used social media himself.

"So, I wasn't sure if I was supposed to kick out on 1 or 2—" Joey was saying, leaning forward eagerly.

Mike quietly said, "Kayfabe."

The table went silent. Joey looked confused but followed everyone's lead, his question dying mid-sentence. I noticed a fan approaching our table, smartphone in hand.

"Hey guys, awesome show tonight!" The fan—a regular

whose name I could never remember—grinned broadly. "Mind if I get a quick picture?"

"Sure thing, buddy," Jim switched instantly to his public persona, throwing an arm around the fan's shoulders while raising the championship belt for the selfie.

After a few minutes of small talk and autographs, the fan wandered back to the bar, satisfied with his interaction.

Joey waited until the fan was well out of earshot. "What just happened?"

"I'll explain later," I said.

After a while, most of the fans left. Joey, Mike, Jim, and I were still at the table. I said, "OK, Joey, you ready to learn something?"

"Yeah! So, what's kayfabe?" he asked. "Everyone froze like someone yelled 'cop.' "

Mike chuckled, the sound rumbling from deep in his barrel chest. "Not far off, kid." He took a pull from his beer, his arm full of tattoos featuring Japanese characters and the Mexican flag. "Kayfabe is our code. It's how we protect the business."

"From what?"

"From them," I explained. "From the marks. We don't discuss finishes in public, we don't break character when fans are around."

"Back in my day," Mike added, "kayfabe was sacred. Heels and babyfaces couldn't even travel together. Jim and I wouldn't be sitting together like this. You lived your gimmick 24/7."

Jim set his glass down on a coaster. "There were rules. Traditions." His salt-and-pepper hair was still neatly combed. "When I came up, we slept, ate, and breathed kayfabe."

"Where did you train?" Joey asked.

"A training camp in Minneapolis," Jim explained. "At the time, it was one of the most disciplined wrestling schools in North America. Technique was everything. You didn't just learn how to do the moves—you learned why they worked, the psychology behind them."

Mike snorted. "While Jim was learning the perfect wristlock, I was in Tijuana getting my head kicked in for forty pesos a night." He touched his cauliflower ear unconsciously. "Different education, same business."

"That's... intense," Joey said, looking between the two veterans. "So, it's OK for us to all sit together now?"

"Things have changed," I acknowledged. "But some of it still matters. What happens behind the curtain stays there. If you're in the middle of a feud, it's best to avoid hanging out where the fans can see you. Stuff like that."

"And when you said 'kayfabe'..."

"It means shut up, someone's listening who shouldn't be," Mike said.

Jim leaned forward. "Luke's right. Shit has changed. But certain fundamentals remain. Respect for the craft. Protecting your opponent. Technical excellence."

"But knowing when to throw all that out the window and just give the crowd what they want is also a skill," Mike countered, winking at Joey. "Sometimes the perfect technical match isn't the one that draws money."

"That's where we disagree," Jim said, though his tone remained friendly. "I believe excellence will always draw in the long run. And shortcuts lead to shortened careers."

Joey looked between them, trying to process these conflicting philosophies.

"So, which is right?" he asked me.

I shrugged. "Both. Neither. Depends. Jim's approach might work perfectly in front of a crowd full of smart marks. Mike's might save your ass in a rowdy bar show where the crowd wants blood."

"I agree. It's important to read the crowd," Jim said. "I've seen great technical matches put audiences to sleep."

"Never yours, though," Mike laughed.

They both turned to Joey, who looked overwhelmed.

"Look," I said, stepping in, "what they're both trying to say, in their own way, is that this business is harder than it looks. What works in Tokyo might bomb in Tijuana. What Jim learned in Minneapolis might not apply in the places where Mike started."

Mike nodded, gesturing with his tattooed hand. "Exactly. You take what works and adjust on the fly."

"But always respect the basics," I said.

"And the guys who came before you," Jim added firmly.

"On that, we agree," Mike said, raising his glass. Jim clinked his against it. Joey and I did the same.

Joey took a swig of his beer. "I love wrestling."

"Kid's a natural, Luke. Told you."

A crash from across the bar interrupted our moment. Glasses clattered, and heads turned toward the commotion. Lady Liberty —still in her street clothes but unmistakable with her red-tipped blonde hair and dark skin—was standing between her boyfriend and Trent, palms pressed against both men's chests.

"I said back off," she warned, voice carrying across the suddenly quiet bar.

Trent raised his hands in mock surrender, but his posture remained challenging. "Just being friendly, Amber. Tell your boy here to lighten up."

Her boyfriend—a compact guy with tattoo sleeves and a day job at the local auto shop—wasn't backing down. "You put your hands on my girlfriend's ass," he growled.

Darlene, the owner, moved quickly from behind the bar. "Knock it off," she warned, dish towel slung over her shoulder.

Mike was quiet. "Should we handle this before Stan hears about it?"

I stood up and walked over between Trent and Amber. "What's going on?"

"Ask him," Amber's boyfriend jerked his chin toward Trent. "Can't keep his hands to himself."

Trent slurred. "Just appreciating talent. That's what this business is about, right? Identifying... assets." His eyes ran down Amber's body.

"You're drunk, Trent," I said firmly. "Time to call it a night."

"I'm not drunk," he mumbled. "But I'll go. Anyway, nobody's paying to watch women pretend to fight. They just like staring at your tits—"

Amber's eyes narrowed dangerously. "Fuck you. Asshole."

The boyfriend moved forward, but Jim stepped between them. "Not worth it, man," he said. "He's drunk. Let him go."

Trent's attention shifted to Jim. "Oh, hey, champ—" his words slurring.

Mike appeared at Jim's shoulder, his presence alone a warning.

Trent looked at the assembled group, calculating his odds. "Whatever. Place is dead anyway." He tossed some bills on the table and backed away.

As he left, Amber's boyfriend wrapped a protective arm around her waist. "That guy is trouble," she said.

I turned to Jim. "Thank you."

He shrugged. "We don't need that shit in here. I like this place."

Mike clapped Joey on the shoulder. "And that, kid, is lesson two of the business. Some guys never learn the difference between heat and just being an asshole."

TEN

"Was that thunder?" Stew seemed panicked as he stuck his head in Stan's office.

"I think so. Maybe. It's supposed to rain today." I went back to studying the electric bill that Stan had left out, which had doubled this month. Another loud thunder clap roared across the warehouse.

"Do you think there might be a tornado?" He was white as a sheet.

"I doubt it. Just a little thunderstorm."

Another thunderclap, louder than before. I got up to look out the door. "Yeah, it's raining pretty good now. But it'll be OK, Stew. No need to worry. Stew?" I turned around and he was gone.

Stan was pissed when he walked in. His shirt soaked, white hair dripping from the downpour outside. "This damn rain can kiss my ass!" Even his shoes seemed to be leaking.

Mike wasn't far behind him. "Holy shit, boss, what happened?"

"Oh, go fuck yourself," Stan said as he wrung excess water from his shirt.

Mike laughed harder while I tried to keep a straight face. "Well, at least ole Stew is dry. I think, anyway. I guess I don't know what the conditions are under the ring."

"What?" Stan asked.

"Yeah, I just saw him roll under the ring. I said, 'Stew, what the hell are you doing?' and all he said was 'Tornado!' "

"Mike, you're so full of shit." Stan had been taken for a ride by Mike so many times before.

Mike crossed his finger over his heart. "Scout's honor."

I headed into the ring room to check on Stew.

"Stewart?"

"Under here."

"What are you doing?"

"Well...I don't like tornadoes, Luke."

"Well, it seems to have calmed down now. You can come out. It's safe." I lifted up the ring apron and saw his face. Beet red.

"I'd love to. I really would. But right now, I'm stuck."

"What do you mean, stuck?"

"Well, I think... I mean... I guess I swelled up."

"You swelled up?" I was incredulous.

"Yeah. Once I got under here, I think I got bigger somehow and now I can't get out. You aren't gonna tell the boys, are you?"

I paused. "Yes, Stew, I am going to tell the boys. Number one, we're going to need their help to get you out of here. And if we don't, you're going to be lying here while they start bumping around in the ring and you'll most likely be killed. But also... this is the funniest thing I've ever seen. How can I not tell them?"

It had taken four guys and a lot of baby oil, but Stew emerged unscathed. His dignity would recover, too. Eventually.

Stan hunched over a legal pad, scribbling notes and crossing things out with enough force to tear the paper.

"Stan?" I asked, leaning against the doorframe.

Stan grunted without looking up. "If it's about Friday's card, I'm working on it."

"The boys just want to know what they're doing."

Stan looked up, irritation flashing across his face. "What's the hurry? They booked elsewhere? Double-dipping on me?"

"No," I lied, knowing at least three of our guys were working shots for other promotions on their off nights. "They just like to know."

Stan snorted. "When I was coming up, half the time we didn't know who we were working until we got to the building. Most of the time, we just called the match in the ring."

There was no point reminding him that "when he was coming up" was a different era with different expectations. When Stan got nostalgic, it was best to just ride it out.

"Jim's asking," I said, knowing that invoking our newly crowned champion might get Stan's attention. "Wants to know who's challenging him first."

Stan tapped his pen against the legal pad. "No title defense this week."

I raised an eyebrow. "Really? But that ladder match was really hot."

"Exactly. Let it breathe. Build anticipation for his first defense."

It wasn't terrible logic. "So what's the main event then?"

Stan shuffled through his notes. "Jim and Trent versus the Nightmare Express."

"Trent?" I couldn't hide my surprise.

"Yep. It's time. And Jim can give him a little rub."

I took a deep breath. "What about the rest of the card?"

"Still working it out." Stan ran a hand through his thinning hair. "It's just the same fucking guys over and over again."

"Brad's back this week." He'd been out of town for the last few shows.

Stan nodded absently. "Could work with Joey maybe."

"Yeah. That'd be good," I agreed. "Kid's been busting his ass."

"That's the problem with this business," Stan said, leaning back in his chair. "Busting your ass only gets you so far. It's about connecting with the crowd. Having star quality." He shuffled through some papers. "Trent is gonna be a star."

I kept my expression neutral. "He's athletic."

"Athletic?" Stan repeated. "The kid's a natural. He moves like he was born in the ring."

"When he bothers to show up for training," I pointed out.

Stan waved this off. "All the good ones have an attitude at first."

This wasn't true, but there was no point in arguing.

I chose my next words carefully. "The guy needs humility, Stan. He needs to learn how to lose, right?"

Stan studied me, then shrugged. "Yeah, I know. I know."

ELEVEN

THE LOCK on my apartment door stuck a little. I jiggled the key, pushed with my shoulder, and it gave way with a reluctant groan. Home sweet home.

I flicked on the lights and surveyed the apartment. Mail had piled up on the counter—mostly bills and credit card offers. Dust covered the coffee table. The plant by the window—a birthday gift from Mom three years ago—had finally died, its brown leaves curled in surrender.

I dropped my laptop bag on the couch and opened the refrigerator. Inside were two beers, a half-empty container of week-old takeout, and a bottle of Heinz ketchup. I grabbed a beer and shut the door.

The remote was wedged between the couch cushions, right where I'd left it two nights ago. I turned on the TV and sank into the couch. I scrolled through Netflix, then Hulu, then Amazon Prime. Hundreds of options, and nothing held my attention for more than thirty seconds. A new true crime documentary. Pass. A sitcom everyone at work talked about. Maybe later. A wrestling documentary I'd already seen twice.

I paused on that one, then continued scrolling. Even in my downtime, I couldn't escape the business.

My phone buzzed. A text from Stan:

Need ring announcer for Friday. Regular guy called in sick. Can you handle it?

I typed back: *Sure,* and set the phone down. Another night, another hat to wear.

The phone buzzed again. An email notification, not Stan this time. I almost ignored it until I saw the sender: Mark Ellison. My oldest friend. My best friend, once upon a time.

Luke,

It's been a while, man. Saw your name pop up on Facebook memories today—that camping trip to Lake Millwood, ten years ago. Can't believe it's been that long.

Anyway, I'm reaching out because we're having a reunion of sorts. Remember our old band, Structural Damage? Jesse found all these recordings we made in his garage, and we thought it might be fun to get together, maybe jam a little for old times' sake. Nothing serious, just for laughs.

Let me know if you're interested. We're thinking the 18th, around 7 PM at Jay's place.

Hope you're doing well,

Mark

I stared at the email. *Structural Damage.* Four guys with more enthusiasm than talent, playing covers in dive bars around town. I'd been the bassist—not because I was particularly good, but because nobody else wanted the job. I hadn't touched my bass in... five years? Six?

The 18th was a Friday. We had a show that night. Every Friday night.

I closed the email without responding. What would I even say? *Sorry, can't relive our glory days because I'll be giving out match times to sweaty men in spandex?*

My gaze drifted to the corner of the living room, where my bass case leaned against the wall. Next to it sat my hiking boots, untouched since that Lake Millwood trip Mark had mentioned. I used to love those weekend hikes—the solitude, the quiet, the simple pleasure of putting one foot in front of another without overthinking it.

When was the last time I'd done anything just for the simple pleasure of it?

I looked around the apartment. The walls were bare except for a framed poster from one of our biggest SWP shows five years back. No photos. No art. Nothing personal except for a shelf of wrestling DVDs and books.

Even my furniture was the kind of stuff you buy when you're just passing through. A couch from a discount warehouse. A coffee table that came in a box. A TV stand that wobbled if you put anything on the left side.

The dating app icon on my phone caught my eye. I'd downloaded it nine months ago, after Mike's persistent encouragement. *You need a life outside the business, Luke. Someone to go home to at night.*

I'd set up a profile, swiped a few times, even matched with someone named Claire who seemed nice enough. We'd exchanged a few messages, and then Stan had called with another crisis. I'd meant to reply to Claire later, but later never came. She'd probably unmatched me by now.

The TV droned on in the background, some reality show I wasn't watching. I took a swig of beer and tried to remember the last time I'd invited someone over. Had anyone ever seen this apartment besides me? The maintenance guy who fixed the shower last winter, maybe.

Stan again:

> Maybe that guy from the building would be a good announcer? The one with the limp. He's been bugging me to get involved – and I'm sure he'd work for free.

I replied: *OK*, knowing that was not a great idea but if it got me off the hook, I was open to anything. I'd filled in once or twice in the past but wasn't great. But I worked cheap and was reliable —sometimes that was all that mattered to Stan.

I scrolled through more streaming options, settling on a science documentary where Neil deGrasse Tyson explained the cosmos. He described how massive objects bend space-time, pulling everything around them into their orbit.

I found myself wondering what a life would look like outside the gravitational pull of Stan Weizenschmidt.

I finished my beer, turned off the TV, and headed to the shower. Tomorrow would be another split day—IT job till five, warehouse by six, home by ten if I was lucky. Rinse and repeat.

As I passed the bass guitar, I ran my fingers along its dusty case, feeling the shape of it beneath the worn leather. For a brief moment, I considered opening it, seeing if my fingers still remembered how to find the notes.

Twelve

The locker room stank of Icy Hot and sweat. The overhead lights buzzed like they might give out any second, casting everything in a sickly fluorescent glow. Three bulbs had already burned out, and Stan hadn't asked the building to replace them. He said it "added ambiance." What he meant was that dim lighting made it harder to see the holes in the ring canvas.

Trent stood in front of a mirror that hung on the wall, admiring his reflection as he flexed. Twenty-four years old and built like he lived in the gym.

"You gonna make out with yourself, or are you gonna get dressed?" Mike called from across the room. A few of the boys chuckled.

Trent smirked. "Jealousy's a disease, old man. Get well soon."

Mike rolled his eyes and went back to lacing his boots. He was thirty-eight years old with knees that popped like bubble wrap every time he stood up. He'd been doing this longer than Trent had been alive, and his body was a mess—a surgically repaired shoulder, lower back that seized up when it rained, and a right ear that looked like it had been put through a paper shredder.

Stan was somewhere—checking on pre-sale tickets or bossing around the girl who worked the concession stand—and the boys were getting restless. Bell time was in forty minutes, and we still didn't have a finalized card.

Joey sat in the corner, stretching. I'd spotted him getting dropped off earlier in the parking lot, sharing a quick embrace with someone in a Honda before heading inside. He was always punctual, always professional—everything Trent wasn't.

"Luke," Joey called over, his voice low, "any word on my match tonight?"

I shook my head. "Stan's busy. But we'll know soon."

The curtain burst open, and Stan rushed in, raindrops spattering his shoulders. He had that wild look that usually meant trouble for me.

"Luke, the damn sign blew over out front. I had to go out there and put it back up. Get one of the security kids to check on it later."

"Sure," I made a note on my clipboard. "I'll take care of it."

"Listen up," Stan barked, not bothering with pleasantries. The room fell silent. Say what you will about Stan, but the man knew how to command a room. "We've got three hundred and twenty-seven people out there. That's fifty more than last month, and I want to keep that momentum going."

I caught Mike's eye across the room. He gave me a knowing look and mouthed "two-seventy" with a subtle head shake. Classic Stan—inflating the numbers when announcing them to the boys, deflating them when payday came around.

"Card's mostly the same as we announced," Stan continued, "but I'm making a few changes." He gestured to me, and I flipped to a clean page on my clipboard, pen poised. "Joey, you're opening with Stew but as 'The Enforcer.' Borrow someone's hood if you don't have your own."

Joey nodded, lips pressed. He was stuck in the opening match again and in a mask, too. The kid didn't complain, but I could see the disappointment in his eyes.

"Trent, you and Jim are tagging against Mike and Bad Brad before intermission."

"Before?" Jim said, not complaining but surprised.

Stan's eyes narrowed slightly. "Yes. After the tag match, I want Trent to turn on Jim. Heat it up. Then Trent," he pointed at him, "you're wrestling Jim next week in the main event. Title match."

The room went still. Every eye turned to Trent, who didn't try to hide his smirk.

"I need that angle to be hot—really hot. Do it right and we'll sell a ton of pre-sale tickets before the end of the night."

Jim didn't say a word to Stan, but he turned to Trent. "Let's talk about the finish. I'm thinking you hit me with a spear and then some sort of submission. A figure four maybe?"

Trent nodded eagerly. "That works. Or I could hit you with the spear, and then the powerbomb."

"Yes to the spear," Jim said. "But let's skip the powerbomb. My back's been acting up. I can sell the figure-four real good and make you look strong."

"Whatever you want, man," Trent said. He wasn't listening.

Stan's eyes lit up. "I want real heat there. Trent, you need to establish yourself as a killer. Someone the fans will pay to see get his ass kicked."

"So, we're turning him heel," I clarified.

"Yep," Stan said. I didn't bring up the humility thing again.

Some guys struggled to be the bad guy out there. But Trent was a natural heel. It was probably the right call. I just didn't like it.

Jim looked concerned. "Just be careful with my back on that spear. It's not a hundred percent."

"I'll be gentle," Trent said.

"No, you won't be gentle," Stan corrected. "You'll be safe.

Make it look brutal but this is a work. There's a difference. We need real heat, the kind that makes people want to see Jim get his hands on you next month."

Stew and Mike exchanged glances across the room. They'd both been around when a tag team nearly caused a riot last year, getting a drunk fan so worked up he tried to climb over the security ropes. That incident had ended with a rushed backstage meet-and-greet during intermission to prevent a lawsuit, and Stan firing the tag team after the show.

"Don't overdo it," I said to Trent. "Get heat, but don't cross the line."

"I know what I'm doing," Trent replied dismissively.

"All good?" Stan asked, looking between Jim and Trent.

They both nodded.

"Alright," Stan clapped his hands. "Let's be safe out there."

As Jim squeezed past me, he gave my shoulder a gentle reassuring pat.

"Do I get a raise?" Trent asked Stan, that smirk still on his lips.

Stan snorted. "Let's see how you draw first, kid."

"Fair enough. But when I pack this place next month, we're gonna talk numbers."

He turned to leave, but Stan called after him. "Trent . . ."

He looked back.

"Don't fuck this up."

I excused myself and headed down the hallway toward the bathroom. The Armory had just one set of facilities shared by both performers and audience. It was always an awkward dance for the boys—trying to maintain kayfabe while standing shoulder-to-shoulder at the urinal with the same fans who'd just been screaming for your blood.

The bathroom was mercifully empty when I entered, but my solitude lasted only seconds before the door swung open behind me. I kept my eyes forward.

"Hey, Luke," came a familiar voice.

I glanced sideways to see Al Price taking his place at the urinal next to mine. Al was at every show, front row, always in the same Black Sabbath t-shirt. He was what we called a "smart mark"—a fan who knew wrestling was predetermined but loved it anyway. He took pride in knowing the terminology and behind-the-scenes dynamics, which the internet had made more accessible to the fans.

"Hey, Al."

"Just saw that new guy is debuting tonight," he said casually, as if discussing the weather.

I winced internally. Someone in the locker room must have already posted about it. Maybe Trent himself.

"Don't believe everything you read, Al."

He chuckled. "Fair enough. Listen, Stan's booking has been solid lately. That ladder match with Jim was full of old-school psychology. Beautiful stuff."

"Glad you enjoyed it."

We stood silently next to one another while I finished up. I went to wash my hands.

"Enjoy the show," I replied, reaching for a paper towel. "Should be a good one."

"Always is." Al grinned.

The tag match was going exactly as planned. Trent and Jim worked well against Mike and Bad Brad. The crowd was into it, appreciating the contrast between Jim's veteran technical style and

Trent's raw power. Even with his injured back, Jim was giving it his all.

The match reached its planned climax. Jim hit his signature spinebuster on Bad Brad, but instead of going to the top rope or the elbow drop, he tagged in Trent. Trent dove off the top, landed a gorgeous leg drop, and the referee's hand struck the mat for the three-count.

The crowd cheered as Jim raised Trent's hand in victory. The heel team rolled out of the ring, selling defeat as they headed up the ramp. This was the moment—the planned turn where Trent would attack Jim and cement himself as the number one contender for the title—without ever winning a match.

Jim turned to Trent, offering a congratulatory handshake. Right on cue, Trent slapped Jim's hand away and shoved him hard into the ropes.

The crowd reacted with shocked gasps that turned to boos. Jim, the respected veteran, looked appropriately surprised and betrayed. Classic storytelling.

Trent grabbed Jim by the hair and threw him into the turn-buckle with real force. Jim bounced off and stumbled forward. This was where they'd planned the spear, then the submission hold.

But that's not what happened.

He hit the spear, not causing any injury but looking like a million bucks. But instead of the agreed-upon figure-four leg lock, Trent pulled Jim to his feet. He put Jim's head between his legs and hoisted the champ up for a powerbomb.

Even if I'd been near the ring, there was nothing I could do.

Trent drove him down with vicious force. Jim hit the mat with a sickening thud. The crowd went silent for a beat, then erupted in outrage.

Jim lay motionless, trying to catch the breath that had been knocked out of him. His face twisted in pain as he tried to roll to his side.

Trent played to the crowd, flexing and taunting them as their boos intensified. He was getting the heat Stan wanted alright.

Stan went to ringside, concern on his face as he slid into the ring to check on Jim. Trent backed away, posing and yelling at the crowd. He slid out of the ring and started up the ramp.

"Get him out of there," I called from behind the curtain to two of our trainees acting as security. Trent was still playing to the crowd. Too much. "Now!"

I watched nervously to see if Jim was going to get up while Trent came through the curtain. I shook my head in disgust.

What was Stan thinking?

THIRTEEN

I HADN'T BEEN to my mother's house in months. I told myself it was because of my schedule, but really, I just didn't know what to say to her anymore.

She lived in the same small house I grew up in, a place that smelled faintly of lemon cleaner and old books. The TV was always on in the background, set to whatever cable news channel was ranting the loudest that day. This morning, though, she was watching some preacher talking about the end times. Also ranting. Loudly.

When she opened the door that Sunday afternoon, she squinted at me for a second, like she wasn't sure if I was real. Then she pulled me into a quick hug. "Well, look who decided to show up."

"Hey, Mom." I stepped inside, hands in my pockets.

"Coffee?"

"Sure."

The kitchen was exactly as I remembered—yellow counter-tops from the '80s, faded wallpaper with small crosses woven into the pattern. A framed Bible verse hung above the sink: "As for me and my house, we will serve the Lord." The letters perfectly straight, just like everything else in her world.

She poured two cups, setting mine down at the kitchen table. I stared at the deep brown liquid, aware of how exhausted I was.

"Your shirt is wrinkled," she noted, smoothing her own well-pressed blouse. "Don't you have an iron at home?"

"Been busy," I muttered, ignoring the sting of her observation.

"So," she said, sitting across from me. "How's wrestling?"

I exhaled. "Same as always. Stan's still Stan. The guys are still breaking their backs for fifty bucks and a hot dog."

She shook her head. "And yet you're still there."

I didn't answer. Instead, I sipped my coffee.

She leaned forward, resting her arms on the table. "You know, I used to enjoy watching wrestling with your father, back before you were born."

From what I knew, Mom had always hated wrestling and complained about it whenever Dad and I watched. Now she was rewriting history, like she did with so many things.

I looked up. "Yeah?"

"He loved it. Stan 'The Man' was his favorite. Thought he was larger than life." A small, sad smile crossed her face. "I remember when you were little, you used to talk about wanting to meet him. Guess you got your wish."

"Yeah." I didn't tell her that as it turns out, meeting your heroes is overrated.

From the living room, the preacher's voice rose in pitch, something about sin and redemption. My mother's eyes flickered toward the sound, then back to me, as if making a silent comparison.

"I saw one of your flyers," she said, emphasizing the word like it was something distasteful. "Someone from church left it in the fellowship hall. All that violence. Is that really how you want to spend your time? What you want to be known for?"

It wasn't a new question, but it never failed to make me feel sixteen again.

"It's a job, Mom."

"You have a job. A good one. With benefits." She tapped her finger on the table. "Mrs. Wilson's son just made director at his company. He's a year younger than you."

And there it was. The inevitable comparison to someone else's son who was doing better, achieving more, living up to expectations. Dad had shielded me from the worst of it when he was alive, drawing her critical gaze to himself instead.

I opened my mouth, then closed it again. There was nothing else to talk about.

She sighed. "You remind me of your father, you know."

I tensed. "Is that a good thing?"

"He was a good man." Her words sat heavy in the air between us, laden with unspoken qualifiers. Good, but not ambitious enough. Good, but not successful enough. Good, but never quite enough.

"Seeing anyone special?" she asked, changing subjects with practiced ease.

I rolled my eyes, setting the mug down. "I should get going."

She didn't try to stop me. "Come by more often, Luke."

I stood up and took my coffee to the sink, careful to put my mug where she'd want it—then realizing it wouldn't matter.

"Oh, I found this the other day. Thought you might want it." She handed me an old VHS tape labeled in my father's handwriting. "Stan vs. Koslov 1986." Hours of matches he'd recorded that she was finally discarding.

I thanked her and stepped outside, videotape in hand.

Fourteen

Monday morning, I sat in my car outside the office, hands gripping the steering wheel like I was trying to crush it. I finally opened the door. It was still dark as I walked into the building.

Eric waved me into his office the minute he saw me.

His office was small but neat, his desk empty except for a few framed photos of his wife and kids. He motioned for me to sit, and folded his hands on the desk.

"Listen, I'll get right to it. You're talented. One of the best problem solvers we have. But your commitment? It's slipping. And people have noticed."

I stayed quiet.

Eric sighed. "Look, I get it. Everyone has passions outside of work. But this wrestling thing... it's interfering. You missed an important server issue yesterday. I had to pick up the slack."

He continued. "Upper management is talking about restructuring soon. There's a senior position opening up. It comes with a significant pay bump." He paused, letting that sink in. "You could be in the running. But only if I see real commitment."

I should've jumped at the chance. Instead, all I could think about was making sure we were ready for Friday's show.

The VHS tape sat on the passenger seat during my drive to the warehouse. I'd left work early. Eric's words about commitment and priorities echoed in my head, but I pushed them aside. I needed space to think. The warehouse was the only place that felt right.

I arrived an hour before anyone else. I flipped on the lights and made my way to Stan's office where the ancient VCR was connected to a small TV. We'd used it for years to review tapes from aspiring wrestlers or study footage from other promotions. These days everything was digital, but I missed the charm of the old tech.

The machine made a mechanical groan as it accepted the tape. I sat in Stan's creaky chair and hit play.

Static filled the screen, clearing to reveal a grainy image of a packed arena. The timestamp in the corner read 06/14/1986— nearly forty years ago. This matched the label. My father had meticulously written dates, venues, and featured matches on the tape's container.

"Ladies and gentlemen," an announcer's voice crackled through the TV, "our main event of the evening. Introducing first, from Moscow, USSR..."

The crowd erupted in boos as a massive figure strutted down the aisle, wearing a red singlet emblazoned with a hammer and sickle. Victor Koslov. Young, muscular, with a thick black beard and a permanent scowl. He shouted something in mock Russian.

"And his opponent..."

The boos transformed to cheers instantly.

"...from Chicago, Illinois... STAN! THE MAN! WEIZEN-SCHMIDT!"

The camera panned to the entranceway as a young Stan emerged, arms outstretched to absorb the adulation. He was leaner than I'd ever seen him, with a full head of blond hair and a confident swagger. He wore trunks featuring an American flag, playing up the Cold War rivalry.

This was the Stan my father and I had admired, the one I'd grown up watching. The differences between that vibrant performer and the man I knew were pronounced.

The match itself was a masterclass in storytelling. Victor played the cheating heel, using dirty tactics whenever the referee looked away. Stan was the resilient hero, fighting back. They moved with a synchronicity that only comes from extensive experience working together. But even with that chemistry, everything they did felt authentic. Believable.

"These two know each other so well," the play-by-play announcer noted. "Former tag team champions, now bitter rivals. You'd never know they were once the best of friends both in and out of the ring."

"Wrestling changes relationships," the color commentator replied. "Especially when championships and money get involved."

"And you should never trust a Russian anyway." I winced at the xenophobia, a staple of '80s wrestling.

I was so engrossed in the match that I didn't hear the warehouse door open. Only when the office door creaked did I look up to see Stan himself standing in the doorway, staring at the screen.

"What are you watching?" His voice was quiet.

I fumbled for the remote. "Sorry, I just—my mother gave me this tape. I didn't think—"

"No, leave it." Stan stepped into the office, eyes fixed on his younger self executing a beautiful dropkick. "I haven't seen this match in years."

On screen, Victor was recovering, grabbing a foreign object from his boot while the referee was distracted.

"He was always good at that," Stan said, almost to himself. "Making it look like he'd pulled something from his boot. There was nothing in his hand."

Stan watched himself. I was fascinated by the softening of his face.

"You two were tag partners before this, right?" I asked, though I already knew the answer.

"For three years. The Cold War Express, we called ourselves. Victor with his fake Russian gimmick and me playing the American hero." He chuckled. "Funny thing is his family was from Pittsburgh. He's never been within a thousand miles of Russia."

On screen, young Stan was mounting a comeback, the crowd on their feet as he fought through Victor's offense.

"We were good," Stan said.

"What happened between you two?"

Stan's expression hardened. "What always happens. Money and women." He pointed at the screen. "This was about six months after he turned on me. Made more money as enemies than we ever did as a team. Until we couldn't stand each other anymore for real."

I studied his face, trying to separate fact from fiction.

"I heard it was something about stolen earnings," I prodded. "And his wife?"

Stan's eyes snapped to mine. "Who told you that?"

"The dirt sheets."

Stan stared at me before turning back to the screen. "Victor always had a big mouth." His jaw tightened. "I never stole from him. We had an agreement about outside bookings. He's the one who started hiding payouts."

"And his wife?"

"Marilyn." Stan's voice softened. "She was our valet for a while. Things got complicated." He shook his head. "Ancient history now."

On screen, the match reached its climax. Stan hit his finishing move—a modified piledriver he called the Chicago Crusher—and pinned Victor to thunderous applause. The camera lingered on his victory celebration, the pride and joy on his face as he held his arms aloft.

"You were really good," I said.

"I was the best," Stan replied without modesty. "Victor too, though I'd never tell him that." He reached over and hit the stop button, freezing the image of his younger self mid-celebration. "Anyway, that was a different time. Different business."

The tape ejected with a mechanical whir. Stan picked it up, turning it over in his hands with unexpected gentleness. "Your dad gave you this?"

"My mom found it when she was cleaning. Dad recorded all your matches."

A flicker of emotion registered on Stan's face. "Nice." He handed the tape back to me.

"I should digitize this before the tape deteriorates completely."

I knew he didn't really understand what I said, but he was too proud to ask questions. He glanced at his watch. "Boys will be here soon. We've got work to do."

"How's Jim doing?" I asked as Stan headed for the door.

Stan paused. "Called this morning. Says his back's stiff but nothing torn. He'll be out this week, maybe next."

"And Trent?"

The softness from moments ago was completely gone. "What about him?"

"You're still gonna push him after that?"

"Trent generates heat. Heat means ticket sales." Stan's voice had that tone—the one that meant the discussion was over.

74

FIFTEEN

The ring rattled as Stew took another bump from Joey, landing with a heavy thud. He exhaled hard but started getting up, moving slower than he probably wanted to. Trent was leaning against the ropes.

"You sure you wanna be taking those, big man?" he said, loud enough for everyone in the warehouse to hear. "I mean... at your age?"

A couple of the younger guys chuckled nervously. Stew just smiled, like he always did. "I might be old, but I can still go."

Trent let out a dramatic sigh. "Yeah, yeah, no doubt. Just saying, it's kinda wild, right? All these years, still here, still in the same ring, still setting up chairs. Never got the belt. Never got the call. Still running drills with the rookies." He glanced at Joey, nudging him. "I mean, can you imagine? Sticking around that long just to be a punching bag?"

Before Stew could respond, Mike shoved Trent—hard—with both hands, right in the chest. Not enough to knock him flat, but enough to send him stumbling back into the corner.

"You're gonna shut your mouth," Mike said.

The entire warehouse went silent.

Trent blinked, more surprised than hurt. "Hey, I—"

Mike grabbed his jaw, gripping it just tight enough to make a point. "No. Shut. Your. Mouth."

Trent swallowed.

"You don't talk like that to the guys who paved the way for your dumb ass to even *be here*." His voice was low but sharp. "You don't *disrespect* someone who's taken more bumps than you ever will. And you sure as hell don't run your mouth about a guy who could stretch you six ways to Sunday if he felt like it."

A long pause.

Trent finally jerked his head free, trying to regain his swagger. "Dude, relax, I was just messing around—"

"You think this is a joke?" he snapped. "You think being in this business is a right? It's not. It's a privilege. And guys like Stew, guys like Jim, they earned it. They paid their dues, they bled for it, they broke their bodies for it. And what the hell have *you* done?"

Mike stared Trent down for another few seconds before finally stepping back. "That's what I thought." He turned, pointing at the younger trainees. "Any of you ever talk like that? You won't make it to next week."

Silence.

Trent wiped his mouth. "Damn, alright, alright. Message received."

Mike didn't respond. He just turned back to Stew and patted him on the shoulder. "Let's go, big man. Run it again."

Stew gave a small nod and reset for another bump. He always smiled. Always let things roll off his back. But he hadn't made eye contact with anyone since Trent had insulted him.

I spotted Jim walk in. "What just happened?"

"Mike took advantage of a teachable moment."

Jim nodded.

I asked, "How are you feeling?"

"Not great."

"Did you go to the doctor?"

"What do you think, Luke?"

"You probably should."

Jim shrugged, then immediately regretted the movement. "I've hurt worse. I'll work through it." He reached into his gym bag and pulled out a small container of homemade liniment—something he'd been mixing himself for years from a recipe he learned somewhere on the road. A sharp herbal smell filled the air as he applied it to his lower back with the same methodical precision he brought to everything.

"You talk to Trent?"

"What's there to talk about? Kid went into business for himself, could've seriously injured me. Didn't even apologize afterward—just kept saying how 'electric' the crowd reaction was."

Stan had pulled Trent aside after the show, supposedly to discipline him, but I'd overheard most of it. The "punishment" was a joke—a half-hearted lecture about "respecting veterans" followed by praise for the heat he'd generated. By the end, Stan was practically congratulating him.

"Stan's got him in the main event with you this Friday," I said. "I told Trent to keep it simple. No powerbombs, no unplanned spots."

Jim snorted. "You watch—he'll try to do whatever he wants. Stan will let him get away with it for whatever reason." He carefully recapped his liniment. "But I won't."

After a pause, he continued. "I had to cancel a job inspection this morning because I could barely get out of bed."

Jim rarely mentioned his shoot job. Like most of the boys, he kept his wrestling and professional lives carefully separated.

"I'm so sorry," I said.

"It happens," Jim replied, his tone making it clear the subject was closed. He checked his watch—the same reliable Timex he'd worn for as long as I'd known him. "I just stopped by real quick before dinner."

Jim's weekly dinners with his son were sacred—the one commitment he never broke, not even for wrestling. The ritual had taken on even more importance after his wife Maggie passed away seven years ago; it was their way of maintaining family connection when everything else had fallen apart.

"Just so you know, some of the boys are already talking about taking bookings elsewhere if Trent's going to be the focus," Jim continued, bringing the conversation back to business. "Nobody wants to be the next guy he decides to hurt."

That was concerning news. If we started losing reliable veterans like Jim, the whole roster would suffer. But before I could respond, the warehouse door swung open, letting in a blast of air along with a face I'd only ever seen on local TV.

SIXTEEN

I RECOGNIZED Tony DiMarco from his commercials. He was heir to DiMarco Auto Group, the largest car dealership in the county. His ads featured him standing in front of shiny new sedans, promising "deals your father would approve of," a wink to the fact that everyone knew he'd inherited the business.

Wearing pressed khakis and a polo shirt with his dealership's logo embroidered on the chest, he looked out of place here. He couldn't have been more than twenty-five.

"Hi there!" he called out. "I'm looking for Stan Weizenschmidt. Is he around?"

I stepped forward, positioning myself between DiMarco and the ring. "He's in his office. Can I help you with something?"

DiMarco's eyes wandered past me, taking in the ring, the wrestlers, the entire operation with undisguised fascination. "I'm Tony DiMarco," he said, extending his hand. "From DiMarco Auto Group? I'm a huge wrestling fan."

I shook his hand, noting the firm grip of someone who'd read about the importance of handshakes in a business book. "Luke Anderson. I handle operations here."

"Great to meet you, Luke! I've been coming to shows for a few months now. You guys put on a hell of a product."

Before I could respond, Stan emerged from his office, glancing at DiMarco with disinterest. "Luke, I need you."

"Mr. Weizenschmidt!" DiMarco stepped forward eagerly. "Tony DiMarco. It's an honor to meet you. I was in the front row of your show last Friday. That main event was incredible."

Stan gave him a perfunctory handshake, already looking past him. "Thanks for coming." The dismissal was clear, but DiMarco either didn't notice or chose to ignore it.

"I was hoping to talk business with you. I have some ideas about taking your promotion to the next level."

"We're in the middle of training right now."

"Oh. Well, is there a better time to talk?"

"Luke handles the business side of things."

Without waiting for a response, Stan walked back into his office. DiMarco stood there for a moment, not expecting to be brushed off.

"He's, uh, very focused during training," I offered. "What did you want to discuss?"

DiMarco recovered quickly. "Is there somewhere we can talk privately?"

I led him into the weight room. "What's on your mind?"

DiMarco leaned forward. "I want to invest in the promotion. Become a partner."

I kept my expression neutral. "We're not looking for partners."

He smiled and cocked his head sideways. "You've not even heard my proposal yet."

I sighed, but relented. "What exactly did you have in mind?"

"Well... I've noticed a few things that... that could be enhanced."

"OK?" I was trying not to be defensive.

"Yeah! I could help with finding better venues, professional lighting, maybe even local TV coverage. I've got capital to invest from the dealership. We could take this promotion to the next level."

The warehouse roof leaked when it rained, and our lighting setup was ancient. A financial infusion wouldn't be the worst thing for us.

"What's your experience with professional wrestling?" I asked.

"I've been a fan my whole life. I've seen every Wrestlemania. I follow Dave Meltzer and listen to all the podcasts. I know what works and what doesn't."

Internally, I rolled my eyes.

"Look, Stan's the man. I get it," he insisted. "He would handle the creative side while I handle the business side. It'll free him up. Plus, I've got the resources you guys need."

"I handle the business side." I don't know if he could hear the edge in my voice or not.

"Oh, I don't want to take anything away from what you've done, Luke. It's great!"

He looked around the warehouse at the worn mats, the secondhand equipment, the patch in the canvas that needed replacing. We both knew the truth.

"What kind of percentage were you thinking?" I asked.

"Fifty-fifty seems fair," DiMarco said without hesitation. "Given the capital I'd be putting in."

I managed not to react, though the figure was laughably high. "And what would your role be day-to-day?"

"Marketing, primarily. Better venues, handling promotions, media coverage." His eyes lit up. "I've got connections at the local TV station. We could get a weekly spot, like the old territory days."

There was something almost endearing about his enthusiasm if it weren't so obnoxious to my old-school sensibilities.

"Stan's very particular about the business, but I can see potential benefits in additional resources."

DiMarco beamed. "So, you'll talk to him about it?"

"I will. But I should warn you—Stan's been doing this a long time, his way. He's not big on change. Or outsiders telling him what to do."

"All I want is a chance to prove what I can bring to the table," DiMarco insisted. "I respect Stan's knowledge of wrestling. That's why I came here instead of trying to start something on my own."

He handed me his business card. "Here's my direct line. Call me anytime to discuss. I really mean anytime—this is an opportunity I'm serious about."

I took the card. "I'll talk to Stan and get back to you. Maybe you should come to the show on Friday. After it's over, we might be able to sit down with Stan when he's not in the middle of training."

"I'll be there," DiMarco said. "Front row again."

As DiMarco headed toward the exit, I made my way to the ring, where Stan was sitting in a chair, watching two students work on a chain wrestling sequence.

I sat down next to him. "He wants to invest in the promotion. Become a partner."

Stan didn't take his eyes off the wrestlers. "Uh huh."

"New venues, better marketing, maybe a local TV spot. He's got connections apparently."

"And what's he want in return?" Stan asked.

"Half the business," I replied.

Stan's head snapped toward me. "Half?"

"Yeah."

Stan shook his head. "Finish up here," he said to the trainees. "Five-minute water break, then we're doing hot tag drills."

Stan walked into his office. I followed.

Once I shut the door, he exploded. "The nerve of that little prick! Half my business? Half?" He paced the small office. "What is it with these money marks? They watch a few episodes of Raw and think they know the business."

"I know. But some of his ideas aren't terrible," I offered.

"Doesn't matter how good his ideas are," Stan snapped. "You know how many guys like him I've seen? Rich kids who think wrestling is cool, want to play promoter until they realize it's actual work. Then they're gone, and you're left picking up the pieces."

"He does have resources," I pointed out. "And the warehouse roof is leaking again."

Stan glared at me. "So you think I should take his offer?"

"No," I clarified. "Half of the business is ridiculous. But maybe there's some middle ground. We could use a sponsor, if nothing else."

"He doesn't want to be a sponsor," Stan countered. "He wants creative control. They always do. Let him get comfortable and before you know it, he'll be suggesting gimmicks, finishes, who should get the push. He probably wants to be my next champion for fuck's sake!"

"I told him to come to the show on Friday," I said. "Thought maybe we could talk more then."

Stan ran a hand through his thinning hair. "Now I'll have him breathing down my neck all night."

"I'll run interference." I promised. "But maybe just hear him out first? Not for a partnership, but maybe a sponsorship deal? DiMarco Auto presents Friday Night Wrestling?"

"Fine," Stan relented. "I'll listen. But the second he starts talking about creative decisions or suggests that he get in the ring himself, I'm done." He looked at me sternly. "And don't you dare tell him I agreed to anything in advance."

Seventeen

The Armory looked different in the hours before a show. Stripped of the chairs and crowd noise, it was just what it was: a former National Guard base turned community space with bad acoustics and flickering fluorescents. The boys were setting up the ring when I arrived, four hours before bell time. Mike and Jim directed traffic, making sure the younger guys weren't slacking. Stan unpacked the concession stand supplies from the closet the building let us use as their only weekly tenant.

"Canvas looks like shit," Stan muttered beside me, eyeing the faded surface with its barely concealed patch job. "Need to replace it before someone catches a toe and breaks their neck."

"I'll add it to the list," I replied, scanning my clipboard. We had a dozen equally pressing needs and a budget that couldn't cover half of them.

That's when I spotted him. Dressed in designer jeans that had never seen manual labor and an Oxford shirt with the top two buttons undone. DiMarco was standing at the edge of the ring, chatting with Stew and one of the newer trainees whose name I could never remember.

"What the hell is he doing here?" Stan hissed, following my gaze. "Show doesn't start for four hours."

"I told him to come," I said. "I didn't specify when."

"Well, he's getting comfortable, isn't he?" Stan watched as DiMarco laughed at something Stew said, slapping him on the back like they were old friends.

"I'll handle it."

As I approached, I caught fragments of DiMarco's conversation. "...and that spot with Michaels and the Undertaker at WrestleMania 25? Pure art. That's the kind of storytelling you just don't see anymore..."

"Luke!" DiMarco turned, spotting me with a wide smile.

"Hi," I said. "You're here early."

"Wanted to see how it all comes together," DiMarco replied, gesturing to the ring construction. "The behind-the-scenes stuff."

Stew and the trainee took the opportunity to slip away, returning to their setup duties.

"It's pretty mundane, really," I said.

"Still cool to see," DiMarco insisted. "I was just telling the guys about this idea I had for your entrance setup. With the right lighting package, you could transform this space. I know a guy who does concert setups—"

I interrupted him. "We need to focus on getting ready for the show."

"Right, right, of course," he agreed. "But maybe after the show I could buy them all a round? Get to know the talent?"

From across the room, I could feel Stan's eyes boring into the back of my head. "They'll be headed to The Wing Place," I said. "Like always." I paused, and added, "That's where all the fans go after our shows."

DiMarco seemed ready to ask yet another question when Mike approached. "Need a couple extra hands on the apron," he said to me, pointedly ignoring DiMarco.

I was grateful for the interruption. "Why don't you come back closer to bell time? Your tickets will be waiting at the door."

"I was hoping to talk to Stan," DiMarco said. "About my proposal? You did mention it to him, right?"

"I did," I confirmed. "But tonight's going to be busy. Maybe after the show."

DiMarco's enthusiasm dimmed. "Of course. Business first." He surveyed the hall. "So much potential here. You guys just need the right support to take it to the next level."

As soon as he was gone, Stan was at my side.

"That little prick is evaluating my operation," Stan growled. "Like he's doing us some favor."

"He's enthusiastic," I said. "And he's not wrong about the lighting. This place looks like a morgue under these fluorescents."

Stan snorted. "If I want advice, I'll get it from someone who's actually worked a match." He looked toward the half-constructed ring. "Keep that asshole away from my wrestlers."

Three and a half hours later, DiMarco returned with two of his buddies. They were all dressed in business casual attire, sipping coffee from an upscale downtown shop I'd only been to once. They settled into their front-row seats while DiMarco nodded to some of our fans who likely recognized him from his television commercials.

"He's back," Brad observed, stretching near the entrance curtain. "With reinforcements."

"I see him," I said. "Don't worry about it. Focus on your match."

Brad nodded, but several other wrestlers sized up the outsiders. Stan emerged, spotted DiMarco, and immediately turned to me. "Tell him I'm busy all night," he instructed me.

"We should be civil."

"I'm always civil," Stan replied. "And always busy on show nights."

As fans filtered in, I checked on Chuck at the music table. DiMarco waved enthusiastically from the front row. I gave a perfunctory nod and acted busier than I was.

Eighteen

Stew dug through a battered duffel bag, muttering curses under his breath.

"Everything okay?" I asked, setting down my clipboard.

"Luke, we got a big problem."

"What?"

"My basement flooded last night. Water main break or something." He held up his bag. "The only gear that didn't get soaked was this old stuff from storage. From, uh... a while back."

I peered into the bag and saw the issue. Neon green and electric pink spandex gleamed under the lights.

"Can't you borrow something from one of the boys?" I suggested.

Stew shook his head. "Whose stuff is gonna fit me, Luke?" He held up the singlet. "This is all I've got."

"Well," I said carefully, "it's better than wrestling in your street clothes."

Fifteen minutes before showtime, the neon strained against Stew's oversized midsection, creating an unfortunate muffin-top effect. His matching pink and green knee pads barely fit his massive legs, and the boots–once white, now yellowed with age—were laced so loosely they threatened to fall off with each step.

"Don't say a word," Stew warned as Double Trouble began to snicker. "Not one damn word."

Mike simply said, "We've all been there, brother."

When Stew turned around, the back view revealed the true horror–the singlet had ridden up dramatically, creating the most severe wedgie I'd witnessed in fifteen years of independent wrestling.

"Stew," I said discreetly, "you might want to... adjust your back situation."

He reached around, felt the problem, and his face fell. "Oh God." He tugged at the fabric, which stretched but snapped back into its unfortunate position. "It didn't used to do that."

"Maybe it shrunk in storage?" I offered.

"Yeah, that's it," Stew said, though we both knew the real issue was the fifty-plus pounds he'd gained.

When his music hit, Stew stood at the curtain. "I can't go out there like this, Luke. Kids from school might be out there."

"It's too late," I said. "And this is wrestling. Make it part of the gimmick."

"My gimmick isn't 'middle-aged man in too-small spandex,'" Stew groaned.

"It is tonight," I replied, pushing him toward the ring.

As Stew waddled through the curtain, the crowd's reaction went from confused silence to scattered laughter that quickly built into full-blown cheers. Stew leaned into it, flexing his arms and patting his protruding stomach.

"That's right!" he bellowed. "The Starmaker's back and brighter than ever!"

His opponent, The Blade, tried to maintain his menacing scowl but even he was having a hard time keeping a straight face.

The bell rang. Everything went smoothly until Stew

attempted his signature move—a top-rope splash. As he climbed the turnbuckle, the strained singlet reached its breaking point. A ripping sound was followed by Stew's look of horror.

He completed the move, landed the splash, and secured the pin, all while trying to hold his shredded singlet together. The referee counted faster than I'd ever seen him count before, just wanting to get the whole thing over with.

Stew rolled out of the ring, not sure where to put his hands. Finally, he gave up. The crowd gave him a standing ovation as he backed to the curtain, one hand raised in victory, the other clutching the remains of his singlet.

"Never again," he muttered as he passed me. "I'm buying three sets of new gear tomorrow."

I couldn't stop laughing.

"Shut up, Luke," he replied, but with a hint of laughter. "And if anyone took pictures, I want them deleted."

The crowd was on their feet before the bell rang. Trent's music hit first—a pounding hip-hop track he'd insisted on using instead of the options I'd presented him.

His muscles were oiled to a sheen. The crowd's reaction was immediate. Loud boos cascaded from the stands, with scattered cheers from the few annoying fans who thought it was cool to cheer for the heels.

"Making his way to the ring, weighing in at two hundred and thirty-five pounds... Trent! 'THE FUTURE' HOWWWWARD!"

The Future? That nickname was news to me.

I looked over at Stan, who was watching from near the concession stand. He was stone-faced, but attentive.

Trent strutted down the aisle, jawing with fans with brazen

bravado. He slid into the ring and climbed the turnbuckle, arms spread wide, soaking in the attention.

"He's enjoying this too much," Mike stood beside me.

"Yep," I replied.

The jeers intensified as Trent posed, which only seemed to fuel his performance. He was playing the heel role to perfection, antagonizing the crowd with every gesture.

As Trent's music faded, the arena fell silent for a beat before Jim "The Hammer" Tanner's entrance theme—an old Metallica tune—blared through the speakers. The crowd erupted again, this time with enthusiastic cheers as the champion made his way to the ring, title belt slung over his shoulder.

"And his opponent, the reigning, defending heavyweight champion of the world... JIM! THE! HAMMER! TANNNNNERRRR!"

Jim worked the crowd like the veteran he was, high-fiving the kids in the front row, nodding at the regulars, and stopping to flex for a group of women who hollered as he passed.

I noticed the slight stiffness in his movements, the careful way he climbed the steps instead of hopping onto the apron. His back was still bothering him from the powerbomb incident; that was real. But he'd taped himself up thoroughly before the match to remind the fans about the injury—and the betrayal.

The contrast between the two men couldn't have been starker: Trent, all raw athleticism and youthful arrogance; Jim, the seasoned professional with two decades of ring psychology and respect etched into every movement.

Jim started cautiously, testing Trent with basic lockups and fundamental holds–the veteran feeling out his opponent while protecting his injured back. Trent was following Jim's lead at first, matching his methodical pace and showcasing his technical ability.

DiMarco and his friends watched from the front row. I saw

him leaning in to whisper observations to his companions. He was studying the product, just as he'd studied the setup earlier.

Ten minutes in, the pace picked up. Jim had worked Trent into the corner and was delivering his signature chops. The crowd counted along as red marks formed across Trent's chest.

Trent took the punishment like a pro, selling each blow with increasing intensity. When Jim came in for the next shot, Trent raked Jim's eyes. The champion wasn't ready for it, and the abrupt —and unplanned—cutoff threw him off. Trent unleashed a flurry of offense that Jim sold despite not fully expecting it.

"That pussy bailed on Jim's chops," Mike hissed.

"Tell me about it," I said.

It seemed like the match was back on track. They hit the spots they'd planned–Jim's backdrop, Trent's dropkick, an exchange of near falls that had the crowd on the edge of their seats.

But as they approached the finish, Trent started to rush. He was supposed to wear Jim down with a sleeper hold, giving the champion time to recover before his comeback. Instead, Trent transitioned directly to his power moves, cutting out the rest hold entirely.

As a result, Jim was blown up—breathing heavy, face flushed. Being blown up could be dangerous. Once you stopped breathing, you stopped thinking, and since wrestling was as much mental as it was physical, that was a problem.

As Trent continued his assault on the champ, the crowd slowly started to chant "Hammer! Hammer!" Jim was selling all of Trent's offense, but as the crowd got louder, his movements got more intense. Eventually, he stopped selling the moves and his whole body shook as he channeled the crowd. Trent punched him one more time and Jim snapped his head up, sending the crowd into a frenzy.

The Hammer blocked the next punch and threw one of his own. Again. He backed Trent up into the ropes and shot him off, hitting him with "The Sledgehammer," a double axe handle to the chest.

Trent took the bump and fed back up for another offensive move by the champion. Finally, just when it seemed like Jim had things handled, Trent grabbed the referee by the shirt and pulled him into the middle of the action.

The referee went down. Jim went to check on him and Trent grabbed the heavyweight title belt. Just as they'd discussed, Jim turned around and Trent hit him in the head with the gold championship. He tossed the title to the corner, lay on top of the fallen hero, and the referee came to just in time to count One . . . Two . . . Three!

Mike was disgusted. "Really? Luke, did you know he was putting the belt on this kid?"

"Nope." Another creative decision Stan didn't bother to tell me about

Trent grabbed the belt and posed on the turnbuckle. He yelled to the referee, "Get Jim out of here." The ref rolled Jim to the floor and helped him to the back while Trent soaked in the boos.

The audience was ready to riot. So was I.

NINETEEN

I HADN'T SPOKEN to Stan yet. He didn't like being questioned. And it was his company; he could do whatever he wanted. But still... putting the belt on this kid already?

I threw a few empty water bottles in the trash in the locker room, while a trainee took down the curtain. I spotted DiMarco out by the ring. I took a deep breath and walked toward him.

"Hey, Luke. Hell of a show tonight. That title change? Pretty electric."

"That was the idea," I replied. He didn't need to know that I was as surprised as he was.

Behind us, the trainees and some of the wrestlers—including Jim—were tearing down the ring. Meanwhile, Trent was in the corner taking selfies with his new championship belt, posing from different angles to catch the light.

"I was hoping to catch Stan," DiMarco said, eyes scanning the room.

"Stan's pretty tied up on show nights."

DiMarco's gaze settled on Trent. "That new champion's got something special, doesn't he? Real star quality."

"Yeah. Stan knows talent when he sees it."

DiMarco nodded. "So, I've worked up some projections. Some numbers that I'd like to run by him. Think he could spare five minutes?"

"I'll ask. Wait here."

I found Stan, who was counting cash from the concession stand, separating bills into neat little piles. I waited for him to finish a stack before interrupting.

"DiMarco's waiting for you," I said in a low voice.

"Why?"

"You know why. He wants to talk business."

Stan peered over my shoulder at the waiting DiMarco.

"I told him you're busy. But he's persistent."

Stan exhaled—not his usual irritated breath, but the sigh of a man dealing with an unwelcome guest. "Give me two minutes to finish here."

I returned to DiMarco. "He'll be over in a minute."

DiMarco straightened his collar, looking like a hopeful job applicant waiting for an interview. "Great. That's great."

Stan appeared moments later, his promoter's smile firmly in place—the practiced expression he reserved for sponsors and venue managers.

"Tony!" Stan extended his hand. "Some show tonight, huh? Hope you enjoyed it."

"Absolutely, Mr. Weizenschmidt. Incredible work." DiMarco pulled a folded sheet from his pocket. "I've been thinking about our discussion and put together some projections—"

"Tell you what," Stan interrupted, taking the paper and tucking it into his back pocket without a glance. "Tonight's not ideal for business talk."

"Of course, I understand—"

"Why don't you give us your number?" Stan continued. "Luke will set something up next week when things settle down."

I recognized the maneuver.

DiMarco brightened, mistaking dismissal for progress. "That would be fantastic!" He handed Stan a business card. "I'm available whenever works for you."

"Great." Stan handed me the card without looking at it. "Luke will coordinate. Maybe Wednesday or Thursday?"

"Either works for me," DiMarco said.

"Perfect." Stan clapped him on the shoulder. "Now if you'll excuse me, I've got payouts to handle."

Stan walked away, opened his ledger book, and extracted a handful of envelopes as if DiMarco had ceased to exist.

DiMarco turned to me. "Wednesday or Thursday then? What time should I come by?"

I knew Stan had no intention of meeting him. "I'll check his schedule and call you."

"Looking forward to it," DiMarco said.

He shook my hand and then made his way over to Trent for a selfie.

I was never calling him.

TWENTY

"YOU MISSED QUITE A SHOW LAST NIGHT," Mike said without preamble. It was eight AM, which meant something had gone very wrong or something happened that he knew I'd find very entertaining. With Mike, it was hard to tell.

"What do you mean?" I replied, scrolling through emails on my computer while I balanced my cell phone in the cradle of my neck."I was at the show, Mike."

Mike chuckled. "Not talking about the wrestling show, Luke. The after-party at The Wing Place. DiMarco came and acted like a total starfucker, licking Trent's nutsack all night long."

"Oh Jesus."

"But it gets better. Trent started some shit, and Stew—" He broke off, laughing too hard to continue.

I set my coffee down. "Stew what?"

"Stew became a goddamn legend, that's what."

"Alright," I sighed, leaning back in my chair and putting him on speakerphone. "What happened?"

"So, we're all there, right? All the usual guys. Trent's holding court, showing off that belt, getting DiMarco to buy shots for these two rats."

Ring rats, girls who made themselves sexually available to the wrestlers, were as much a part of the business as the ring itself. Some guys handled the attention with more discretion and class than others. Trent was not one of those guys.

"Anyway, there's this dude at the bar. A big guy, not wrestler big, but gym big, you know? Turns out he's the ex of one of these girls Trent's pawing at."

"Oh God."

"Right? So, this guy's been staring daggers at Trent all night. Finally he comes over. Says something like, 'That's my girlfriend you're groping, asshole.'"

"And?"

"And Trent with his belt on his shoulder says—I shit you not —'Not anymore, she isn't. Championship privileges, brother.'"

I closed my eyes. "No he didn't."

"It gets better. Ex-boyfriend takes a swing. Misses by a mile because he's three sheets to the wind. Trent pops him one right in the mouth. Clean shot. Guy goes down, then gets back up madder than hell."

Mike continued, "Brad and I are moving to break it up. But before we get there, this guy tackles Trent into Double Trouble's table. Drinks go everywhere, glasses are breaking. The girls are screaming, Darlene's threatening to call the cops, and Trent's got this guy in a headlock."

"Where does Stew come in?"

Mike's laughter returned, rich and genuine. "Stew's been sitting at the bar all night, drinking club soda and scarfing down hot wings. Minding his own business. Doesn't even turn around when the fight starts. But then they crash into his stool, and knock his plate over, and he gets buffalo sauce all over his shirt. Man, it was scary. The way his face changed. He stands up—and you know how when Stew stands up at full height, the whole room notices?"

I did. At six-foot-six and nearly four hundred pounds, you couldn't miss him.

"Stew walks over, calm as can be. Picks Trent up by his collar, sets him aside like he's nothing. Then he grabs this other guy, who's still throwing wild punches. The guy takes a swing at Stew—and that's when it happened."

"What happened?" I asked impatiently.

"Stew grabs the guy by his balls."

"He what?"

"Reaches right down and clamps onto the guy's package. Just grabs a hold and squeezes."

I winced. "No shit?"

"The guy starts screaming. High-pitched, like a tea kettle. But Stew won't let go. Brad and I are trying to pull him off, the girls are still screaming, Trent's laughing his ass off, and Stew keeps squeezing."

"How long did this go on?"

"Too long. Maybe thirty seconds? Felt like forever. Darlene's yelling that she's calling the cops, and Stew just looks at this guy, real calm, and says, 'Are you done?' Guy can barely nod, tears streaming down his face."

I massaged my temple, trying to ward off a headache. "And then?"

"Stew finally lets go. Guy crumples to the floor. Stew straightens his shirt—the one covered in sauce—looks around at everyone, and says, 'Sorry about that. Been a long night.' Then sits back down and asks Darlene for another club soda to dab on his stained shirt."

I found myself laughing. That was pure Stew—the sudden explosion followed by calm, like nothing ever happened.

"The guy's friends dragged him out," Mike continued. "Darlene ended up not calling the cops, but she put the broken glasses —and Stew's replacement wings—on Trent's tab. And now Stew's got a new nickname in the locker room."

"Do I want to know?"

"The Nutcracker."

I groaned. "Stan know about this yet?"

"Thought you should hear it first, so you can do damage control if needed."

"Thanks for the heads up."

"Get yourself a beer next time," Mike said. "You miss all the good stuff hiding at home."

I pulled out my phone and texted Stew:

> Heard you made an impression last night.

His response came quickly:

> Sorry, Luke. Guy ruined my favorite shirt. Won't happen again.

Twenty-One

Joey and Stew both got to training an hour early. Joey was fixing a turnbuckle that had a wire sticking out of it, while Stew handed him a pair of pliers. At forty-five, Stew was our oldest active wrestler, still in his security uniform with a name tag that said "Mr. Paul." Most of the students at the local high school where he worked had no idea he transformed into "Stewie the Starmaker" on weekends.

I called out, "Hey, guys. We're actually gonna take the ring apart and rebuild it tonight before training."

"Oh, alright," Joey said. Stew handed him a wrench and together they began loosening the ropes.

"Did Stan talk to you?" I asked Joey.

"He said I'm teaming with Eddie against Trent and Mike this weekend."

"What do you think about that?"

"I'm happy for the opportunity. I like working with Mike a lot."

"Yeah, Mike's the best. Do what he says and lean on him for help with Trent if you need it."

"I know. We'll keep it simple. And don't worry—I'm not taking that stupid powerbomb."

———

Trent had the championship belt on his shoulder when he strolled in to the warehouse. Late again. No one in the history of SWP had ever carried the belt around in their real life. But I wasn't sure where real life started and stopped with Trent.

"Nice of you to join us," I called from my table.

Trent flashed that cocky grin. "Traffic, man. What can you do?"

"Call. Let someone know you're running late."

"I'm here now, aren't I?" He dropped his gym bag by the door and strutted toward the ring like he was making an entrance on pay-per-view instead of showing up for a regular Tuesday training session.

He looked at Joey and Stew and the other trainees who were working on the ring. "You guys mind wrapping this up? I need ring time to work on my moves for Friday."

"They'll be done when they're done," I said, not bothering to look at him. "You're welcome to use the weight room in the meantime. Or you could help them with the ring."

He snorted and wandered off. Joey watched him go, said nothing.

When the ring was put back together, Joey tested it by throwing himself backwards and taking a hard bump. "Feels good, Luke," he said. "I think we're ready."

I gathered the trainees around the ring and ran my hand along the newly tightened top rope. "OK, she's ready. Not only is the base of the ring crucial to your safety, but so are the ropes. You want them firm but with just enough give. Too tight, and they'll mess up your timing when you hit them. Too loose, and they are dangerous for aerial moves." I looked at Joey. "Help me demonstrate?"

He hit the ropes cleanly—back on the middle, arm wrapped around the top. His momentum carried him back in a smooth, controlled arc. The rope vibrated with just the right tension. Then he took another bump, just to be sure.

"That's what we're looking for," I told the trainees. "Doesn't matter how good the moves you do are if the ring itself isn't safe. You need a strong foundation to support everything that comes after. Without the basics—including respect for the business—people get hurt."

Mike walked in and smiled. "You guys listening? Even though Luke doesn't wrestle, he knows more about this business than a lot of people. So, when he speaks you should take notes. Alright, give me two laps around the block." Then he looked at Trent. "Champ, let's talk." The way he said "champ" sounded more like condescension than respect. They walked into the weight room.

As the rest of the trainees headed outside, Stan came out of his office.

"What's that about?" Stan asked, nodding toward the weight room where Trent was now describing something to Mike with dramatic arm gestures.

"Who knows," I said.

"They'll be good. Mike can show him the right way to do things."

"He'd have to want to learn, though."

Stan ignored that and went back into his office.

Mike came over a few minutes later, jaw tight. "Kid wants to do a top-rope powerbomb this Friday. Says it'll be his new tag team finisher. The 'Star Crusher' or some such bullshit."

"And you told him no, I hope."

"Course I did. Told him first of all, the name was dumb because it's too close to Stew's gimmick. Secondly, I'm not sure he can do it without hurting someone." Mike was pushing forty, with a body held together by stubbornness and athletic tape. He'd seen too many careers ended by reckless moves. "Plan is, we'll do whatever Stan tells us for the finish. His old-school ass wouldn't know a Star Crusher from a Spanish Fly."

The championship belt lay on the weight room bench beside where Trent had been lifting. Carelessly tossed like an afterthought. Mike's eyes flicked toward him—posing in front of the mirror, flexing from different angles.

"You think he'll last?" Mike asked.

"I hope not. For all of our sakes," I answered.

"Kid's gonna crash and burn. Question is how many of us he takes with him."

The students returned from their run. Joey walked over to Mike and me. Stan's office door opened. He spotted Trent and he greeted him with a wide smile.

"His golden goose," Mike bemoaned.

"More like a golden pain in the ass," I replied.

Joey laughed.

Stan approached us, beaming like a proud father. "Good news, gentlemen. Ticket pre-sales for Friday are up twenty percent from last month." He continued, "I just got off the phone with Dave Reynolds from Pro Wrestling Quarterly. He's sending a photographer to the show. Says he might do a feature on our champion."

Trent preened, adjusting the belt on his shoulder. "Told you I was money, Stan."

Stan ignored the arrogance and turned to Mike. "You two sorted out the finish for Friday?"

Mike and Trent exchanged a look.

"What do you want us to do, Stan?" Mike said carefully.

"I thought we agreed on the Star Crusher," Trent said, a challenge in his voice.

"The what now?"

"My new finisher. Top rope powerbomb."

Stan considered this. "Can you do it safely?"

"Of course. I've practiced it."

"On who?" I asked sharply.

Trent hesitated. "Well, not on anyone yet. But I've visualized it."

Mike snorted.

Stan waved his hands. "Well, you guys figure it out, Mike. Just make sure the champ looks strong."

Trent looked upset and walked outside.

"Someone needs to get through to him before he hurts somebody else," I said.

"He's young. He'll figure it out," Stan said.

"Until he hurts someone," Mike said. "Again."

Stan waved dismissively. "It'll be fine. You worry too much."

"That's my job," I reminded him. "To worry about the things you don't."

Stan chuckled, clapping me on the shoulder. "And that's why I keep you around, Luke." He wandered back toward his office. Mike watched him go, then turned to me. We didn't say anything. We didn't need to.

I found the belt from the weight bench and walked outside where Trent was vaping. "Is there a problem?"

"No."

"Then why did you storm off like that?"

"I'm good."

"Not as good as you think you are." I handed him his title. "And stop wearing the belt around town. You look like an asshole."

I thought I was the only one still there. But just as I was about to hit the lights, Joey came around the corner, gear bag over his shoulder.

"Thought everyone had left," I said.

"Sorry. I was waiting on my ride."

As we walked outside and I locked the door behind me, a Honda pulled to the curb. A young woman rolled down the driver's side window. Her dark hair was pulled back in a practical ponytail, and she wore a pale blue scrub top.

"Who's this?" I asked.

Joey smiled. "Rachel, this is Luke."

"Hi," she said. There was something striking about her—a quiet confidence, maybe, or the way her eyes seemed to take in everything at once. Joey's whole demeanor shifted when he saw her.

"Nice to meet you," she said, extending her hand across the seat. I leaned into the car. Her hand was soft, her grip firm. "I didn't recognize you without your clipboard."

"You know me?"

"My dad and I come every week. It's our thing."

Joey added, "Rachel's been coming to shows forever. She was in the crowd for my first match. I guess she thought I was hot."

"Oh yeah. Your sweet ass made me overcome with desire," she said dryly. "Get in the car, you goof."

Joey laughed. I did too.

"See you tomorrow?" he asked.

"Where else would I be?"

"Nice meeting you, Luke," Rachel called as I walked to my car.

I opened the door to my Impala. As they drove away, I scrolled through Spotify looking for something that would keep me company on the drive home. I settled on "Long Train Runnin'" by the Doobie Brothers.

As I pulled out of the lot, I wondered if there was anything in my refrigerator worth eating.

Twenty-Two

"Look at this shit," Chuck said, shoving a glossy flyer into my hands as he rushed into the venue. His face was flushed. Our August event, The Summer Sizzler, was three hours away.

"UNIVERSAL WRESTLING ASSOCIATION PRESENTS: SATURDAY NIGHT SHOWDOWN" splashed across the top of the page in bold font. The event was scheduled a month from now at some place called the Millersport Sports Arena.

"Is that the new soccer barn by the highway?" I asked.

"I think so. Can you believe it?"

Then I saw it. At the bottom, in slightly smaller text: "Brought to you by DiMarco Auto Group."

"Where'd you get this?" I asked.

"Walmart parking lot. Every car had one." Chuck adjusted his glasses and threw up his hands. "They're running our territory, man."

I folded the flyer and tucked it into my back pocket. "Don't tell Stan. Not yet."

Chuck nodded and shuffled off to set up the sound equipment.

"Not bad, huh?" Stan said, appearing at my side, gesturing to the packed house.

"Not bad," I agreed. "Let's hope the show delivers."

"It will," Stan said confidently. "Especially the main event."

I glanced toward the locker room where Mike and Trent were presumably going over their tag match with Joey and his partner Eddie Evans. "They sort everything out?"

"Far as I know. Mike will make it work."

The opening matches went well. As promised, Dave Reynolds, the wrestling photographer, had come and had his camera at ringside. His coverage wouldn't mean much as far as attendance goes, but our guys being featured in his magazine would likely lead to better outside bookings.

I watched from the curtain as Joey and Eddie made their entrance first. The crowd loved them, especially Joey, who had become a fan favorite over the last few months, with his 'aww shucks' demeanor and his underdog-like tenacity.

Then came Mike and Trent's entrance. Mike played the grizzled heel veteran, sneering at the crowd. Trent followed with the championship belt held high, strutting to the ring like he owned the place. Most everyone hated him, a few people admired him, but most importantly all of them reacted.

"Kid knows how to make an entrance," Stan murmured beside me. I stayed silent.

The match started smoothly, with Mike and Joey working the early portion. Their chemistry was evident from all those training sessions together–every exchange crisp, every counter believable. When Trent and Eddie tagged in, the dynamic shifted.

Eddie bumped like a pinball, making Trent look like a million bucks.

Stan said, "Eddie can make anyone look good."

For twenty minutes, the match built beautifully. Mike controlled the pace when he was in, Joey took the heat—the part of the match when the heel was in control. Trent would do something underhanded, Eddie would come in without a tag, the referee would go to put him out, and Mike and Trent would cheat. It made the crowd angry every time.

Eventually, Joey made his way over to Eddie for the hot tag. When Eddie came in, he ran offense on both heels, and then it was time for the finish.

Mike and Eddie toppled out of the ring, following a double clothesline over the top rope. That left Joey and Trent alone in the ring.

Joey whipped Trent into the ropes, caught him with a dropkick, then another. The crowd sensed the momentum, rallying behind Joey. Trent regained control with a quick reversal, sending Joey into the corner.

Trent climbed the turnbuckle. Joey looked up, confused. This was not what they had called. But then I could see his face make a split-second decision to just go with it.

Trent stood on the top rope, but Joey knocked his feet off the ropes, crotching him. The crowd roared. Then Joey climbed into position on the second rope. Trent awkwardly gave him a gutshot, which allowed him to put Joey's head between his knees. Joey used his own strength to help Trent lift him into position.

"What's he doing?" Stan whispered.

"I think it's the fucking *Star Crusher*," I sighed.

For a second, everything looked good. Joey was upside down, Trent's arms wrapped around his waist. Then came the descent.

Trent's inexperience showed in the critical moment—he leaned too far forward, lost his balance. Joey, trying to help make the move look good, couldn't adjust in time. Instead of landing flat on his back, Joey's shoulder hit the mat at an awkward angle, and they both tumbled in a tangle of limbs.

The crowd gasped. Trent scrambled to his feet, looking stunned. He quickly covered Joey. The referee made the three-count, called for the bell, and immediately signaled to the back for help.

Trent's music hit. He raised his hands in victory, but his eyes kept darting to Joey, who wasn't moving.

The heels did not break character despite what had happened. But I could see Mike's face whispering furiously at Trent.

I was already on my way to the ring, Stan close behind. The referee knelt beside Joey, checking on him. Joey was conscious, now clutching his shoulder, his face twisted in pain.

"What happened?" I asked, sliding into the ring.

Joey grunted through clenched teeth. "Landed on my shoulder. I think."

From the other side of the ring, Mike grabbed Trent's arm and dragged him toward the back, championship belt forgotten on the ring apron.

Eddie helped Joey to his feet. Joey winced with every movement.

"Can you walk?" I asked him.

Joey grimaced as we eased his arm into a more comfortable position. "Get me to the back."

As we helped him through the ropes and out to the floor, Dave was snapping away furiously with his camera. We all ignored him.

Once behind the curtain, Joey's composure cracked. "Fuck!" he hissed, leaning against the wall.

Mike was already tearing into Trent in the corner. "What the hell were you thinking?" he growled intensely.

Trent's face had gone pale. "Joey called it..." he started weakly.

"Don't you dare put this on him," Mike cut in. "You were told no to that move. Directly told. By me. By Luke. By Stan."

Eddie had followed, carrying Joey's entrance gear. "Got your stuff, man," he said, setting it down carefully. A security guard came back, carrying the belt and awkwardly handed it to Trent. Mike was still yelling.

Stew appeared from another corner of the backstage area, his massive frame holding a bag of ice. "Here, Joey," he offered, holding out a ziploc bag he'd hurriedly filled from his personal cooler. He shifted his weight, looking like he wanted to say more but couldn't find the words. He finally settled for giving Joey's head a gentle pat, his huge hand almost comically careful in its touch.

"Hey, Luke, some chick named Rachel wants to come back here?" one of the security kids called out.

I nodded at the security guard and Rachel rushed in through the curtain. She scanned the room, spotted Joey, and moved straight to him.

"Let me see," she said, no panic in her voice, only clinical assessment. She gently probed Joey's shoulder, ignoring the chaos around her.

Joey grimaced. "How bad?"

"Bad enough. You're coming with me to the ER. You'll need an X-Ray," Rachel replied calmly.

Stan burst through from the curtain. "What the hell happened out there?"

"Your champion did it again," Mike said, jerking his thumb toward Trent.

All eyes turned to Trent, who stood awkwardly against the wall.

"I thought it would work," he said defensively. "We connected in the air. But something went wrong on the way down."

"It's not his fault," Joey said, wincing as Rachel fashioned a makeshift sling from a towel.

"Yes it is," Mike said.

Rachel cut in, her tone making it clear she wasn't asking permission. "I'm taking him to the hospital."

Stan ran a hand through his hair, sighing heavily. "Alright, alright. What's done is done." He looked at Trent. "You. Be at the gym at eight a.m. tomorrow."

Trent nodded.

"Until then, I don't want to hear another word about this," Stan continued. "We've still got fans out there. The show goes on."

With that, Stan stalked off toward his office, leaving us in uncomfortable silence.

Rachel helped Joey toward the exit. "Come on."

Joey passed by Trent on his way out. Trent opened his mouth, but no words came out. He just stood there, looking lost.

I followed Rachel and Joey to the parking lot, carrying Joey's gear bag. "You sure you don't need help?"

"I got it," Rachel replied, not unkindly. "Thanks."

As they drove away, I stood in the parking lot, the distant sounds of the ring being broken down filtering through the building walls. I felt the crinkle of the flyer in my back pocket.

One crisis was about to become two.

TWENTY-THREE

THE NEXT MORNING, I sat on a folding chair, arms crossed, while Stan paced behind his desk.

"He's late," Stan muttered, checking his watch for the third time in five minutes.

"He always is."

Stan shot me a look but didn't respond. We'd been waiting for Trent for twenty minutes. The meeting was supposed to start at eight sharp.

At 8:24, the door opened, and Trent strolled in, wearing sweatpants and a hoodie, looking like he'd just rolled out of bed.

"Sorry I'm late," he said, not sounding sorry at all. "Traffic."

"At eight in the morning? On a Saturday?" Stan asked dryly.

Trent dropped into the other folding chair. "I have ADHD. It fucks me up with time and stuff. I'm sorry."

Stan and I exchanged glances at the rare moment of vulnerability. Or was it just another excuse? It was hard to tell.

"So, what's up?" The kid either had balls of steel or no self-awareness at all.

"What's up," Stan said slowly, "is that you have a problem."

"Huh?"

"You've hurt two of my guys now."

Trent shifted uncomfortably. "Yeah, about that... I really am sorry. It was a mistake. Won't happen again."

"You're damn right it won't," Stan said, his voice hard. "Because from now on, every spot, every move, every damn step you take in that ring will be approved by me or Luke first. Is that clear?"

"Yeah..." Trent muttered.

"And you're going to personally apologize to Joey. Not just a text or a phone call. Face to face."

"When's he coming in?" Trent asked.

"He's not," I said. "It could be weeks before he's cleared."

Trent had the decency to look guilty. "Shit. I didn't know it was that bad."

"Now you do," Stan said. "In my day, if you hurt a guy you went with him to the hospital and you stayed with him. You fucking kids today —" Stan stopped mid-rant and looked at Trent. "And here's what else you're going to do: you're going to apologize to Mike. Mike told you not to do that top-rope powerbomb. You ignored him."

Trent's head snapped up. "But—"

"I'm not finished!"

When Stan got this angry, people paid attention. "Mike's been in this business twenty years," Stan continued, his face reddening. "When he tells you a move is dangerous, you listen. You don't decide you know better because you've been wrestling for five minutes! And so you will not only apologize to Joey and to Mike but to the entire roster and to Luke and to me."

I watched the tension build between them. Stan wasn't just upset about the injury; making him look bad with the boys was unforgivable.

"This is bullshit," Trent muttered.

"Excuse me?"

"I said this is bullshit," Trent repeated, louder this time. "I'm your champion. The one putting asses in seats. And you're treating me like some goof. Because of one mistake."

"One mistake?" I said. Stan put his hand up to cut me off and then he started yelling.

"You're only the champion because I said so. Not because you're hot shit, not because you're Trent Fucking Howard. Because I said so," Stan stood up to meet Trent's gaze. "Don't forget that. I made you what you are. And I can unmake you just as easily."

For a moment, they stared each other down, neither willing to back down. I was ready to step in if things escalated, but I wasn't sure I'd be effective. I'd seen Stan get physical with guys before and it was not something I ever wanted to see again.

"Without me, what do you have?" Trent asked, his voice dangerously quiet. "Just a bunch of old has-beens. Mike's old news. Jim's pushing fifty. Fat Stew? Come on. I'm your meal ticket, Stan. We both know it."

A fury flared in Stan's eyes—an anger even I'd rarely seen. He turned to the wall, and punched a giant hole in it. "Get out," he said, each word precise and controlled.

Trent stalked out without another word, slamming the door behind him.

Stan sank into his chair with a heavy sigh. "Well, that wasn't good."

"Better than I thought, actually," I replied. "At least you didn't kill him."

He looked every one of his sixty-three years. "I think I made a mistake with this kid, Luke."

I answered diplomatically. "You didn't know."

"Yes, I did. You told me. I just..."

"So, do we have a backup plan? Just in case he doesn't show this weekend?"

"It'll be fine. He'll be there. He needs the spotlight, and he knows that without me he doesn't have one. Let's put him with Stew on Friday; he won't be able to hurt that big bastard even if he tried."

"OK."

"And, Luke, I know you know, but I appreciate all you do. Thank you. For... all of it."

I wasn't sure how to respond.

"Just doing my job," I said finally.

Twenty-Four

That afternoon, I stood outside Rachel's apartment door. I waited five minutes before knocking, feeling awkward about crossing some imaginary line between personal and professional. But the image of Joey crashing on the mat wouldn't leave me—that sickening sound, the crowd's stunned silence, his body crumpled at that unnatural angle. I had to check on him.

I knocked twice, the sound faint against the door. I'd already turned to leave when the door swung open.

"Luke?" Rachel stood in the doorway, dark hair pulled back in a messy ponytail, wearing scrubs. Surprise registered on her face before she smiled. "Come in."

"I just wanted to check on Joey," I said, hovering at the threshold. "After what happened."

"He'll be thrilled to see you."

"His mom gave me your address."

"Oh, yeah. She just left, actually. We thought it would be better if someone could keep an eye on him around the clock," she explained. "But she works two jobs and isn't really set up to take care of a patient the way I am. It's nice of you to come by. He's in the guest room. Pain meds have him drifting in and out."

"You just get off work?" I asked, noticing the dark circles under her eyes. I motioned to her name tag, still hanging from her scrub top.

"Just walked in from a twelve hour shift. Luckily, I keep a pair of scrubs in my car since I was already there." I liked the way she spoke. A hint of sarcasm. Like most ER nurses, I guess.

I followed her through her modest living room, with books stacked on an end table, a blanket thrown over the couch, framed photos on the wall.

The guest bedroom was dim, shades drawn against the afternoon sun. Joey lay propped on pillows, his injured shoulder wrapped in medical tape. His eyes fluttered open as we entered.

"Luke?" Joey's voice was groggy but he managed a smile. "What're you doing here?"

"I'm checking on you, man. That was a nasty bump."

"Tell me about it." Joey shifted, wincing. "Doc says I'm lucky. Could've been worse."

"Yeah. Stan had it out with Trent this morning."

Joey's eyes focused. "What happened?"

"Let's just say Trent got the message. Stan really tore into him."

"It wasn't all his fault." His eyes were already drooping. "I shouldn't have let him... Anyway, I'll be back soon as I can. Just need some... rest..."

His voice trailed off as medication pulled him under. Rachel adjusted his blanket, checked the ice pack on his shoulder, then indicated that I should follow her back into the kitchen.

"He keeps saying that," she said as we walked back to the kitchen. "That he'll be back soon. Coffee?" She was already reaching for the pot.

"Sure. Thanks."

She poured two mugs and sat across from me, both hands wrapped around hers like she was warming them. For a minute neither of us said anything. From the guest room I could hear the faint sound of Joey's breathing, slow and medicated.

She turned her mug in a slow circle. "You know he's been doing this since he was sixteen. Backyard stuff. Goofing off with his friends."

I nodded. I'd heard some version of this story from most of the new guys. Untrained, passionate kids playing wrestler doing crazy shit for their friends and families on the trampoline or a home made ring of some sort.

Rachel looked up. "I know it isn't ballet. But man, it's not right, you know? Someone gets hurt and then just... nothing?"

"Yeah."

"I worry about him getting back in there."

It wasn't quite a question either. I looked at my coffee. "He's tougher than most."

She was quiet for a moment. Through the kitchen window, the afternoon light had gone flat and gray. Her calendar hung on the fridge—nursing shifts in blue marker, a dentist appointment, something circled in red I couldn't read from where I sat. A full life, organized and legible.

"Joey told me you've been with Stan's promotion forever," she said.

"Fifteen years, but yeah, something like that."

She nodded slowly, like she was filing it away. "How does your wife deal with it The business?"

The question landed a little sideways. "It's just me."

"Oh. Right." She said it quietly, without pity, which was almost worse. She took a sip of her coffee. "Joey talks about you like you're—I don't know. Like you're the reason the whole thing works."

"Stan's the reason it works."

"That's not what he says." She held my gaze for a beat, then looked down. "Sorry. I don't mean to—" She stopped. Started again. "I've been a wrestling fan since I was a kid. But the more I'm around it... well... it's not always so great, is it?"

I didn't say anything.

"He's good," she said, gesturing toward the guest room. Something shifted in her voice—quieter, more careful. "I think he's genuinely good. And he loves it. I'm not trying to take it from him." She turned her mug again. "I just don't want him to love it more than everything else."

The refrigerator hummed. Down the hall, Joey made a small sound in his sleep.

"He's really good." I drained my coffee and stood. "I should let you get some rest."

She walked me to the door and leaned against the frame, arms crossed.

"Thanks for coming by," she said. "It means a lot that you came."

"Sure."

She started to say something else, then seemed to think better of it. "When he's feeling better, you should come for dinner. Or something."

"Yeah," I said. "Maybe."

She didn't push it. I walked to my car. Behind me I heard the door close, and then the deadbolt turning—the solid sound of domestic normalcy.

I sat in the driver's seat for a minute before starting the engine.

TWENTY-FIVE

A FEW WEEKS LATER AND—PER usual—we were waiting on
the champ to arrive.

"Where the hell is he?" Stan's question hung in the air unan-
swered. Twenty minutes until bell time. And our heavyweight
champion was nowhere to be found.

"I've called him six times," I said, scrolling through my recent
calls. "Straight to voicemail every time."

Stan paced the small confines of the locker room, his face
growing redder with each lap. Three hundred and sixty pre-sold
tickets—our biggest advance in months—all on the strength of
the main event: Trent defending the heavyweight championship
against "Stewie the Starmaker" Paul. They'd been building to this
for weeks, a surprisingly effective replacement feud for the one
that was scheduled with Joey—and it had the fans genuinely
invested. Posters plastered on every shop window in a twenty-mile
radius.

And now our champion was MIA.

He'd done what he was told. He showed up, apologized to
Mike. He gave a contrite speech to the locker room. Just like Stan

told him. Maybe with less sincerity than we'd hoped. Still, he did it.

Mike looked at us both and said, "Fuck Trent. He's a piece of shit. He's probably worried Stan's going to take the belt off of him tonight." That had not been the plan, as far as I knew.

"Anyway, you still good to drive up to Chicago tomorrow, Luke?"

"Yeah," I nodded. "But let's get through tonight first."

"We need to make a decision," I said to Stan, checking my watch. "We need a main event."

Stan slumped onto a folding chair. "Stew's going to be pissed."

The door swung open, and for a split second, I thought it might be Trent, sauntering in with some half-baked excuse about car trouble or a missed alarm or maybe blaming his ADHD again.

But it was Stew himself, already in his ring gear, coming in from a smoke.

"Where's he at?" he asked, glancing around the tense room.

I exchanged a look with Stan. "We can't reach him."

Stew blinked, realization dawning. "You're kidding me. He's no-showing? Tonight?"

No one answered. The silence was confirmation enough.

"Unbelievable," Stew muttered. He ran a hand through his hair, thinking. "So, what's the plan? Who am I working?"

"We're working on it."

"Well, somebody better do something," Stew said, his usual good nature fraying at the edges. "I've been telling everybody I know to come to this show. My sister's out there with her kids."

"We'll figure it out," I assured him, though I wasn't sure how. Our options were thin, without a complete reworking of the card.

Stan stood up, his expression shifting from despair to determination. "Here's what we do. Mike, you OK working twice?"

"Sure, boss," Mike replied.

"And I'll close the show with the official announcement about the tournament for the championship."

"Tournament?" Mike asked. "What tournament?"

"The one I'm announcing tonight," Stan said with an edge of impatience.

Classic Stan—conjuring a solution out of thin air.

Once we were alone, Stan said, "This is about that apology, isn't it? He's throwing a tantrum because I called him out."

"I mean, it's been a few weeks now. I thought everything was cool. Maybe he thinks you're putting the belt on Stew."

"God, I would never—" Stan interrupted his own train of thought. "Well, he can kiss my ass. Nobody's irreplaceable. Not even Trent Fucking Howard."

Something had been gnawing at me—a suspicion I'd been reluctant to voice. With Trent's no-show, I couldn't keep it to myself any longer.

"Stan, there's something you should know."

He looked up, wary. "What now?"

I handed him the flyer. He glanced at it. "What's this? Competition?"

"Yeah."

Stan waved dismissively. "There's always these fly by nights popping up. Am I supposed to be worried?"

"It's Tony DiMarco."

That got his attention. "The car dealership guy? What does he know about wrestling?"

"Enough, I guess? He's running the old soccer barn across town. And he's smart enough to run on Saturday night instead of directly against us on Friday."

Stan studied the glossy flyer, his expression darkening as he traced the name at the bottom with his finger: DiMarco Auto Group.

"This is bullshit," he said, but his voice lacked conviction. "Some money mark thinking he can play promoter because I didn't let him in my sandbox."

"Maybe," I conceded. "But he's got money to burn."

"So what? Let him waste his money. I've been running this territory for twenty years. We've got a loyal audience, the best wrestlers—"

Stan stopped abruptly.

"You think Trent...?"

It wasn't really a question.

"I think it's possible," I said carefully.

Stan crumpled the flyer in his fist. "Son of a bitch. That ungrateful little—" He cut himself off, breathing heavily. "No. He wouldn't dare. Not with our belt."

And there it was—an even bigger problem. Our heavyweight championship—the physical belt itself—was expensive, custom-made, the one piece of our operation that looked truly professional. And it was in Trent's possession.

"Stan—"

"No," he repeated firmly. "He's just making a point. Showing me he can call the shots. He'll turn up tomorrow or Sunday, tail between his legs, looking for a second chance." He straightened his tie, composing himself. "We do the show tonight, announce the tournament, act like everything's under control."

I wanted to argue, to push the issue, but Stan had that look— the one that said his mind was made up, reality be damned. And right now, we had a show to put on.

"I'll go check on Mike and Stew," I said. "Make sure everyone knows what they're doing."

But as I turned to leave, Stan caught my arm. "You going to stake out this soccer barn show tomorrow night?"

"I can't. I'm driving our crew to Chicago."

"Oh, right."

Stan would probably go and sit outside and count the cars in the parking lot. I hoped that was all he'd do.

I wondered if Tony DiMarco had any idea what he'd just unleashed.

Twenty-Six

My Impala groaned as we hit another pothole on I-65.

"Jesus Christ, Indiana," Mike exclaimed from the backseat. "Ever heard of road maintenance?"

"Sorry, I'll try to drive around 'em," I said.

"I wasn't back-seat driving, Luke. I promise." I smiled at him in the rear-view mirror.

Stew shifted in the passenger seat with a series of grunts. At six-foot-six and at least four hundred pounds, he took up more than his share of the available space. We'd voted him shotgun because nobody wanted his knees jammed into their spine for three hours.

"You doing okay up there, big man?" Joey asked from behind him.

"Yeah," Stew said, his discomfort obvious. "This seat doesn't go back any further, does it?"

"Unless you want to sit in Mike's lap, I think you're maxed out."

Mike snorted. "Pass."

The dashboard clock read 11:23 AM. We'd been on the road

since ten, making decent time despite stopping when Stew insisted he needed coffee "or someone was going to die." Fair enough.

I saw Amber's Civic following a few car lengths behind. She had her opponent for tonight's show riding shotgun, with their boyfriends crammed in the back. Neither guy was in the business, and when they climbed out of the backseat at the gas station they both looked miserable.

"Think they'll make it the whole trip without a fight?" I motioned toward the Civic.

"Depends on if Amber's boyfriend makes any more comments about wrestling being fake," Mike replied. "Last time he did that, she made him sleep on the couch for a week."

Joey shifted in his seat, adjusting the sling that still supported his healing shoulder. The discomfort of the long drive was taking its toll, but he still seemed happy to be along for the ride.

"How's the shoulder?" I asked.

"Stiff. But better than last week." Joey rotated it slightly, testing its limits. "Doc says another couple weeks before I can start light training."

"No rush," Mike said firmly. "Shoulder injuries are nothing to mess with." He rolled his neck, working out the kinks. "I'm still feeling last night's double duty."

Stew twisted around as much as his bulk would allow. "You're smart to give it time, kid. Not like me." He patted his massive stomach. "Blew out my knee in '09. Came back too soon, now it's garbage. Same with the back, the ankle..."

"The neck," Mike added.

"The hips. Pretty much my whole body," Stew concluded with a self-deprecating laugh. "At this point, I'm just a collection of parts that don't work quite right."

Joey looked between the three of us, horror and fascination on his face. "Jesus. Why do you guys still do it?"

Mike stared out the window at the passing farmland. Stew

became interested in adjusting the air conditioning. I tightened my grip on the steering wheel.

"I mean," Joey backpedaled, "not like that. I just—"

"No, it's a fair question," Mike said. "Why do we keep destroying our bodies for fifty bucks and a hot dog?" He paused. "For me, it's simple. I don't know who I am without it."

His tone was reflective. "I had a WWE tryout once. In 2008. They said I had potential but needed to work on my look." He snorted. "Code for 'too short, too fat.' So, I kept grinding on the indies, thinking my next big break was just around the corner. Fifteen years later, still waiting."

Joey said, "I didn't know about the tryout."

"Not something I advertise," Mike shrugged. "Anyway, at some point the dream of 'making it big' turned into just... keeping the dream alive at all. Even if it's just in VFW halls and high school gyms."

Stew agreed. "For me, it's the only place I feel... Shit, I don't know. Out there—" he jerked his thumb toward the world beyond the car windows, "—I'm just a fat security guard at a high school. People stare, make assumptions. But in the ring? I'm Stewie the Starmaker. Professional wrestler. I'm somebody. You know?"

I kept my eyes on the road, but I could feel Joey looking at me, waiting for my contribution to this impromptu therapy session. But what could I say? That I stayed because I didn't know how to leave? Because after fifteen years, Stan's little promotion had consumed my identity so completely that walking away felt like a kind of death?

"What about you, Luke?" Joey asked, right on cue. "Did you ever want to wrestle?"

"Me? I just drive the car," I deflected. "And make sure you lunatics don't kill each other."

"No really," Joey said. "You've been around forever. Did you ever want to get in the ring?"

"Not really. I was never the athletic type."

Before Joey could press further, Stew changed the subject. "So, what's the deal with this UWA thing? They're running their first show tonight?"

"Yeah," I confirmed, grateful for the redirect.

"I heard it was that DiMarco guy funding things. Didn't he want to get in bed with Stan?"

"Let's not talk about it," I said.

Joey added, "Rachel's brother works at his dealership. Says he's obsessed with WWE, has replica belts all over his office."

"Great," Mike groaned. "Another money mark living out his fantasy by taking money out of our pockets."

An uncomfortable silence fell over the car. We all knew the reality of someone running against us, even on different nights. Our fan base wasn't wealthy and they'd have to choose which ticket to buy. And when attendance was down, pay was down. It wasn't like Stan was forking over a livable wage as it was. Some nights were lean enough that guys went home with barely enough to cover their gas.

"You think Trent's jumping ship?" Joey asked.

"Hard to say," I replied, though the question of our missing championship belt hung unspoken between us.

TWENTY-SEVEN

"THAT'S how you execute a false tag," I said, pointing to the ring where an old-timer and his partner had just demonstrated textbook technique. "See, they timed it perfectly so the ref wouldn't see it. And hear the crowd. They are pissed. I love that."

Joey was rubbing his injured shoulder, his sling temporarily set aside while we watched the matches. His eyes were fixed on the action, trying to absorb every detail. We'd found a great vantage point—a quiet corner near an unplugged Pepsi machine that the promoter had disabled to boost his own concession sales.

Up next was Mike's match with Stew. "Mike's so smooth," Joey said admiringly. "Guy makes it look effortless."

"Twenty years, man," I replied.

The venue was typical for indie shows in this region. Folding chairs were arranged around the well-worn ring. But the crowd was solid, about 250 paying customers, and they were engaged, responding to each match with enthusiasm.

So far, our crew was delivering. Mike and Stew's match was the third of the night, following Amber's technically sound bout with a woman named Scarlett. The promoter had practically hugged me after their match, gushing about how "you don't see women who can wrestle that good on indie shows."

"See how Stew's playing this?" I said, pointing to the ring where Mike had just tried a shoulder tackle—and failed miserably to move the big man.

Joey's eyes narrowed. "David versus Goliath. I love that dynamic."

"Exactly. Guys with Stew's size have it easy if they know what to do with it."

The crowd was fully invested in the match, the simple wrestling psychology working its magic. While the result was predetermined, the emotional journey was real—and Stew and Mike, despite their chronic injuries, were master storytellers.

"There it is," Joey said as Mike, after trying to knock him down for a few minutes, finally bumped the big man. And the crowd went wild for it. "They've hardly done anything but the crowd is going nuts!"

"I know Stewie's thrilled to be playing the heel for a change."

I noticed Joey rubbing his shoulder again. "Itching to get back in there?"

"It's weird. Like I can almost feel the moves in my body even though I'm not doing them."

"That's how you know it's in your blood, kid," I said.

In the ring, the referee started counting to ten and Mike made it to his feet first. They proceeded into the comeback and Mike hit a massive spinebuster on Stew for the pin. The crowd went wild.

Our boys represented themselves—and Stan—well. The promoter was beaming by the end, already talking about booking us again next month.

"Tell Stan I'd take his guys and girls over anyone else on the circuit," he told me as I collected our pay envelopes. "I'm so sick of sloppy workers who can't even run the ropes properly. Your crew makes me look good." He handed me a stack of envelopes full of cash for the talent. "By the way, what's up with a new promotion starting in your backyard?" he added. "UWA or something?"

I tensed slightly. "Yeah. Their first show's tonight. We'll see if they draw."

"Crazy timing," he remarked. "Almost like they waited until you guys were out of town."

"I'll pass the praise along to Stan. He's proud of these guys."

"He should be," the promoter said. "And I'd use that kid Joey who came along to watch when he's ready to go again. Mike said he's got 'it.' Means a lot that he rode along, just to learn."

I checked my phone, looking for any text messages or updates from home. I wondered if Trent was at the UWA show. If our belt was there.

I had no messages.

As we loaded our gear into the cars, Mike suggested we hit the casino about twenty minutes away before heading back to the motel. "Maybe I can turn this fifty dollars into a couple hundred."

Twenty-Eight

"HOLY SHIT!"

Stew's bellow echoed across the casino floor, drawing glances from the other gamblers near the high-limit area. I hurried over to where he sat frozen in front of a slot machine, his massive frame blocking my view of the display.

"What happened? You okay?"

Stew turned toward me, his face a mask of shock. "I think I just won a jackpot."

I peered around him to see the machine flashing and playing a celebratory animation. "How much?"

He pointed at the screen. "It says eight thousand dollars!"

My eyebrows shot up. "No kidding? Nice one, Stew!"

"Yeah, but..." Stew looked caught between elation and mortification. "I didn't mean to bet that much. I thought it was a penny machine."

"Wait, how much did you bet?" On a dollar machine, max bet was usually around five lines at maximum credits—possibly $50 or $100 per spin. No wonder he looked terrified.

"Jesus, Stew," I laughed. "Living dangerously."

"I almost had a heart attack when I realized," he admitted. "Then the thing started going crazy."

By now, Mike and Joey had joined us, drawn by the commotion. When Stew explained what happened, Mike doubled over laughing.

"Only you, Stew," he wheezed. "Only you could fuck up into a jackpot."

A casino attendant arrived to process the hand pay. While Stew waited, the rest of us drifted toward the bar area. Joey seemed quieter than usual, nursing a soda while Mike and I debated the merits of blackjack versus video poker.

"Everything okay?" I finally asked him. "You've been in your head all night."

Joey sighed. "Just thinking about stuff."

"Wrestling stuff or life stuff?"

"Both, I guess." He fiddled with his straw. "Rachel's got a lead on a job for me at Heartland Products. Her cousin works there."

"Oh?" I kept my tone neutral, though something tightened in my chest. "What kind of job?"

"Assembly line. Good benefits, steady hours. Pays better than the warehouse I'm at now." Joey looked up, meeting my eyes. "A lot better, actually."

"That's... good. Right?"

"Yeah, it is. It's just..." Joey trailed off.

"It's just...not wrestling," I finished for him.

"Right."

"It's tough to make it full time in the business, you know."

"Yeah. I know."

"I mean, I could still train sometimes, still work weekends with Stan. But the schedule would be different. Overtime sometimes. Might miss some training."

There it was—the constant tug-of-war between passion and practicality that every wrestler eventually faced. I'd seen it dozens of times over the years. "Making it" in wrestling meant being able to drop everything and drive somewhere for a last-minute booking in the hopes that you'd get seen by someone important, network with the right guy, and eventually earn a contract that paid enough to live on. A "real" job made that almost impossible.

"You're worried about splitting your focus," I said, understanding.

"But I also need to make a living. Especially if..." He trailed off again.

"If?"

A flush crept up Joey's neck. "If Rachel and I keep getting more serious. I can't exactly raise a family on wrestler pay."

He was right; I'd seen too many wrestlers try to balance family life with the road, watched marriages collapse under the strain, witnessed guys miss their children's milestones while chasing that ever-elusive "big break."

"Look," I said finally. "You've got real talent. Anyone with eyes can see that. But talent doesn't pay the mortgage. Most of these guys have been doing this twenty years and still live paycheck to paycheck. Stew just won eight grand and it's probably the most money he's seen at once in his life."

Joey absorbed this while I continued.

"All I'm saying is, the factory job? That's not giving up. It's being smart. Wrestling will still be there on weekends."

"What if Stan doesn't see it that way?"

A valid concern. Stan had a notorious streak of possessiveness toward his trainees, especially those he saw potential in. He'd been known to freeze out wrestlers who didn't make wrestling a priority.

"Let me worry about Stan," I said. "You do what's right for you."

Joey relaxed. Slightly. "Thanks, Luke. I appreciate it."

"For what it's worth," I added, "the fact that you're even

thinking this way puts you ahead of most guys in the business. Too many chase the dream until it breaks them—physically, financially, personally."

Before Joey could respond, Stew rejoined us, triumphantly waving a big stack of hundred-dollar bills.

"Congrats, big man," Mike said, clapping him on the shoulder. "What are you gonna do with all that cash?"

"Pay off my credit cards," Stew replied without hesitation. "Then maybe get my car fixed. Transmission's been slipping."

"Smart. Boring, but smart," I said.

"That's me," Stew laughed. "Boring but smart. Like when I turned down that ECW tryout in '99."

This was news to me. "You had an ECW tryout?"

"Almost. Heyman liked my size, thought I could be the next 911. But they wanted me to come to Philly. My mom was sick, though, so I said no." He shrugged his massive shoulders. "Two years later, they went bankrupt anyway. Guess boring and smart worked out."

As we settled into our respective drinks, the conversation drifted to speculation about what might be happening at the UWA show. None of us had heard from Stan all day, which was unusual given his tendency to micromanage even when we were in different states.

"Ten bucks says Stan's at that UWA show right now," Mike wagered.

"No bet," I replied. "That's exactly where he is. Outside in his car, fuming, and debating whether to go inside and confront DiMarco."

I hoped he was just sitting in his car.

TWENTY-NINE

I WALKED AWAY from the bar with a fresh beer when I caught sight of Amber sitting at a small table with her opponent, Scarlett.

"Mind if I join you?" I asked.

Amber gestured to one of the empty chairs. "Be our guest. We're just trading war stories."

Joey appeared behind me, a beer in his hand, and pulled up the fourth chair.

"I was just telling her about my first real booking," Amber said, taking a sip of something electric blue. "A tiny bar in Kentucky, crowd of maybe fifty people, promoter tried to pay me with a gas card that had already been used."

Scarlett laughed. "Mine wasn't much better. A high school gym in Missouri, where I had to change in the janitor's closet. I drove five hours and got a whole can of Pepsi and a leftover slice of pizza as my payoff."

"Worth it though, right?" Joey asked.

"It's always worth it," Amber said. "Even when it isn't."

I smiled. Joey nodded.

"When I started," Amber continued, "I had exactly two options for what kind of wrestler I could be—sexy eye candy who couldn't work or tough black girl from the ghetto who wasn't allowed to be attractive." She rolled her eyes. "Like the two were mutually exclusive. Meanwhile, guys got to be anything they wanted."

"Heard that," Scarlett murmured. "First promoter I worked for wanted to put me in a schoolgirl outfit. I was twenty-six."

"That's why I created Lady Liberty," Amber said, straightening slightly. "'When I was a kid, you'd see bra and panties matches and girls who were just there to be gawked at. I'm just glad that my mom introduced me to Madusa and Sherri Martel—women who could go in the ring. Even Moolah, though God knows she had her issues behind the scenes.'"

"So the patriotic gimmick was your idea?" Joey asked.

"One hundred percent. I figured if I was going to be stuck being the 'token female,' I'd at least make it something I could connect with. America is complicated, right? Flawed but with potential. Just like me." She smiled. "Plus, the red, white, and blue gear gets a reaction no matter where you go."

"Smart," Joey said.

Scarlett leaned forward. "We have to be twice as smart. As women, we can't just show up and expect to be taken seriously."

"Exactly. Like tonight—I drove all the way out here, booked this girl"—Amber tipped her glass toward Scarlett—"with my own contacts, then risked my neck in the ring hoping the promoter would pay us what he promised."

"You mean sometimes they stiff you?"

"They try. But it's not my first time, you know. I know how to get what I'm owed. I'm not shy about asking for my money up front if it doesn't feel right."

"Does Stan do that?" Joey asked.

"No. Stan pays. He's difficult in other ways."

"How?"

"He constantly bitches about having girls on the show." Amber didn't hesitate. "Says the crowd doesn't care, that it's a 'specialty attraction' at best. Took me a year to convince him to introduce the women's title, and even then, I had to buy the belt myself."

"To be fair," I interjected, feeling oddly defensive of Stan despite everything, "belts are expensive—"

"I know, Luke," Amber said, her voice firm but not unkind. "But I've been tracking the gate figures for my matches since day one. When I'm on the card, the house is good. I'm over, especially with families and younger girls. But Stan's got this idea of what wrestling is supposed to be, and it's stuck in 1985."

"Well, I'm always glad to see you on the card." It was true. She did draw a crowd. And whenever Amber was around, the boys behaved better.

"Scarlett is booked next week Friday, actually."

"Oh cool," Joey said. "You two had a great match tonight."

Before the conversation could continue, Amber's boyfriend, Kevin, approached the table. He was short, with his Red Sox cap pulled low, tattoos crawling down his forearms. The other guy was tall and lanky with a scraggly beard.

"There you are," the taller one said, his words slightly slurred. "Been looking all over."

Scarlett greeted him with a tight smile. "How'd you do, Ryan?"

"We're both down two hundred," Amber's boyfriend answered, pulling up more chairs. "Table was rigged. Dealer was cheating or some shit."

"Shocking," Amber said dryly. She turned to her man. "Kevin, this is Luke and Joey. You've met them, right?"

Kevin's attention seemed elsewhere. "You about ready to go? We've got a long drive tomorrow."

"We just got another round," Amber said, gesturing to the fresh drinks. "And besides, St. Louis isn't that far."

"Come on, Amber," Kevin said. "It's already late."

I could feel the subtle shift in energy—the men's irritation seeping into the easy atmosphere we'd built. Ryan leaned toward Scarlett, whispering something that made her face harden momentarily.

Joey and I exchanged glances. "We should probably check on Stew," Joey said. "Make sure he's not blowing through that jackpot."

"Good idea," I agreed, standing. "Nice meeting you," I added to Ryan. "And good seeing you again," I said to Kevin, who barely acknowledged me.

"That was interesting," Joey said as we headed toward the slot machines to find Stew. "I didn't know the girls had it so hard."

"Yeah," I said. "I can only imagine what it's like for them."

I looked back one more time. Scarlett was looking at me.

THIRTY

SLEEP WASN'T COMING. The thin motel walls did little to muffle the sounds of passing trucks on the nearby highway, and my mind kept going—tonight's matches, Stew's improbable jackpot win, the UWA, Trent, our missing belt.

After an hour of staring at the ceiling, I gave up and decided to find something to drink.

The vending area was tucked into an alcove at the end of the motel's second floor—a sad arrangement of humming machines bathed in fluorescent light that seemed unnaturally bright at 1:30 AM. I was fishing in my pocket when I realized I wasn't alone.

"Water or soda?"

I looked up to find Scarlett—Amber's opponent from tonight's show—behind me, staring at the Coke machine. She was wearing sweatpants and a faded Green Day concert t-shirt, her red-streaked black hair pulled up in a messy bun. Without the makeup and ring gear, she looked different. More real.

"Water," I replied, finally finding a crumpled dollar. "Can't sleep?"

"Hard to wind down after shows," she said, selecting a Diet

Coke. "Plus, the walls in this place are paper thin. I think the couple next door is either having the world's best time or someone's being murdered."

"Yeah, I can hear them from my room too."

She got her drink. I got mine.

"You can call me Jessica, by the way," she said, leaning against the snack machine.

"Jessica," I repeated. "I'm—"

"Luke," she finished for me. "I know. Amber told me about you. Says you're the reason the promotion still functions."

I shifted uncomfortably. "She exaggerates. Stan is the man."

"But you're the one who makes it all work," Jessica insisted. "I've been in this business long enough to know the difference between who's in charge and who's essential."

There was something disarming about her directness.

"I liked what you said earlier," I admitted. "At the casino. About women having to be twice as smart in this business."

Jessica softened. "Amber's been fighting that battle a lot longer than I have. She's the real deal."

"Still," I said. "It made me feel different about things."

Jessica took a sip of her soda. "That's all any of us can ask for, I guess. To make people feel...something."

I became acutely aware of how close we were standing in the narrow alcove, of the fact that we were alone in this anonymous motel at an hour when normal people were asleep.

"Ryan asleep?"

"Passed out in our room." She looked down at her soda, then back at me with a wry smile. "Let's just say things are... complicated."

I thought about my empty apartment back home. "Oh?"

She studied me. "You're different than I expected."

"How so?"

"I don't know. Most guys I've dealt with in the business are all assholes. You listen when people talk."

I wasn't sure how to respond to that.

"Anyway," she continued, moving slightly closer, "I wanted to thank you for the booking next week. Working with Amber is always good, and I've heard great things about your promotion."

"I'll pass that along to Stan," I said automatically.

Jessica smiled, a hint of mischief in her eyes. "I wasn't thanking Stan."

I became hyperaware of small details—the faint scent of her shampoo, the way her t-shirt had slipped to reveal one shoulder, the pulse visible at her throat.

It had been a long time since I'd been this close to a woman.

"I should probably..." I looked vaguely toward my room, though I made no move to leave.

"Probably," she agreed, not moving either.

I don't know who closed the distance first. Maybe we both did. One moment we were standing apart, the next her lips were on mine, her hands in my hair, my back against the humming vending machine.

When we broke apart, Jessica looked as surprised as I felt. "Can we go to your room?" she whispered.

"Yes."

We walked silently down the breezeway, a careful foot of space between us. As soon as the door closed, her hands found the buttons of my shirt with ease.

"Just so we're clear," she murmured against my neck, "this isn't about bookings or favors. This is just...tonight."

"Just tonight," I echoed. My hands fumbled with her bra strap like I'd forgotten how this worked, like my body had been asleep for years and was just now remembering it could feel things.

"And Ryan...?"

"Don't worry about him," she said firmly.

Thirty-One

The Red Roof Inn disappeared behind us as I merged onto the highway, heading back to Indiana. Stew was still patting the envelope containing his winnings like he was afraid it might disappear.

"I still can't believe it," he said for the tenth time. "Eight grand. From one spin."

"Not a bad payday for pressing the wrong button," Mike said from the backseat.

"Beats getting dropped on your head for fifty bucks," Joey added.

"I don't know what I'd do with all that cash," Mike said, leaning forward between the seats.

Stew's massive fingers tapped the envelope thoughtfully. "Well, I told Luke and Joey that I think I'll pay off my credit cards first. And get my car fixed. But I should get Mom's bathroom redone with those grab bars and the walk-in shower she needs. Been putting that off for too long."

"You still in that house on Maple, right?" Mike asked.

"Yep," Stew confirmed. "Moved back in when she started

getting bad. Supposed to be temporary, but... well... security guard pay only stretches so far."

I'd known Stew had been living with his mother, but I'd never considered how long it had been. The sacrifice quietly made, without complaint, much like everything else in Stew's life.

"What about you guys?" Stew asked, uncomfortable being the center of attention. "What would you do with eight grand?"

"Clear my lawyer bills from the last divorce," Mike said with a humorless laugh. "Or maybe put it toward one of those beach houses in Mexico."

"That sounds great," Joey said.

"Shit." Mike checked his phone. "I need to be back by three. I promised Lizzie I'd take her to dinner tonight before dropping her back at her mom's."

"Your daughter?" Joey asked.

"Sixteen going on thirty. I see her every other Sunday. Her mom moved her out to the west side of the state after the divorce. It's almost two hours one-way." He stared out the window. "Time goes quick though. Even though I only get about five hours with her, it's better than nothing."

The digital clock on the dashboard read 9:17 AM. Mike's phone rang. "It's Jim," he said. "Hammer time! What's up?" He listened for a minute and said, "Wait, this is too good, let me put you on speaker."

Jim's voice crackled through the phone's tiny speaker. "You guys will never guess what went down at the UWA show last night."

Stew perked up. "You went?"

"Hell no!" Jim was adamant. "But you know that fan, Al Price? He was there and filled me in."

"Telegraph, telephone, tell a wrestler," I muttered. "What happened?"

"A lot."

"Tell me," I said. Jim loved taking his time telling a good story —in the ring and out.

"First, as we suspected, Trent was on the show. And he had our belt with him."

"What?"

"Yep. But get this—Stan was there, too."

The car fell silent. Then all at once:

"Oh my God," from Stew. "No fucking way," from Mike. "Shit," from Joey, and a heavy sigh from me.

"He nearly got himself arrested."

I tightened my grip on the steering wheel. "What exactly happened?"

"Well, I guess Stan walked in the front door and DiMarco saw him and headed him off. Apparently, the marquee outside was advertising Trent as defending the belt. You know, OUR belt. And DiMarco was charging a dollar less per ticket than we do, by the way. Anyway, Stan loses it, storms inside, and starts raising hell."

"How bad?" I asked, already dreading the answer.

"Bad. According to Al, Stan marched straight up to DiMarco and started screaming at him. Called him every name in the book. Something about shoving Trent's head up his own ass, threatening to sue them both into oblivion, if they could even walk their pathetic, no-good asses into court. The works."

Stew whistled low. "Oh no."

"Security tried to escort him out, but he kept going. Called DiMarco a 'money mark piece of shit.' Al said everyone in the place could hear it."

"What did DiMarco do?" Joey asked.

"That's the crazy part. Guy stayed calm the whole time. Just waited for Stan to run out of steam, then told him, 'I tried to work with you, Stan. Remember that.' Then had security walk him out."

"And Trent?"

"Oh, he was in the main event. Al said he looked great, had new gear. DiMarco's spending money, that's for sure." Jim paused. "Show was sold out, by the way. Over four hundred people."

"How was the wrestling?" Mike asked.

"Al said it was decent. Not as good as our shows, but solid. Trent went over clean in the middle. Place went nuts."

I stared at the highway stretching ahead, trying to process what this meant for us. Stan's outburst. Trent's defection. DiMarco's successful first show. None of it boded well.

"Anyone else we know on the card?" I asked, dreading the answer.

"It was a bunch of guys from Cincinnati, I think. I didn't recognize most of their names. But Trent defended against "Bulldozer" Bobby Weston. And get this—" Jim's voice lowered dramatically, "—Tony DiMarco himself managed Trent."

"You've got to be fucking kidding me," Mike groaned. "The car salesman's on the show?"

"His promotion, his rules," Jim replied. "Hey, I gotta go. Just thought you guys should know what happened before Stan gives you his version."

After we hung up, the car felt tense, uneasy.

"Stan's going to be on the warpath," Mike finally said.

"Well," Stew said, "training should be interesting this week."

Thirty-Two

By Monday, everyone knew about Stan's confrontation with DiMarco. The boys kept their heads down, worked their drills with unusual focus, and avoided any mention of UWA, Trent, or Saturday night's incident.

Stan himself was absent, having texted me that morning.

Handle training. Busy with legal stuff.
Will explain later.

As Mike supervised chain wrestling drills, I caught his eye across the ring. We were likely thinking the same thing. Whatever Stan was planning was not going to end well.

After training wrapped up, Joey lingered while the others filed out. He'd been watching from the sidelines, taking notes, asking smart questions.

"So," he said, trying to help me roll up the mats with his good arm. "Any word from Stan about what happened?"

"Nothing," I replied. "But he'll have to address it eventually.

We've got a show Friday, and half the roster is wondering if there's even going to be a promotion by then."

Joey hesitated, then said, "Rachel's cousin called. About that job at Heartland. They want me to come in tomorrow. For an interview," he continued, not quite meeting my eye.

"That's good news," I said. "You should go."

"Yeah." He fiddled with the edge of a mat. "It's late in the day so... I might be late to training."

"It's fine."

"It's just... the timing, you know? With everything that's happening, it feels like I'm abandoning ship."

I straightened up, fixing him with a direct look. "Listen to me. You take that interview. You aren't abandoning anything."

"I don't think Stan will see it that way."

"I'll handle Stan."

Joey looked relieved. "Thanks, Luke."

My phone buzzed with a text as I started the engine of my car.

Where are you?

Just leaving training.

Stay there.

Stan pulled into the lot in his Cadillac. He opened the door and said, "Let's go in and sit down."

I unlocked the door and pulled up a folding chair. Stan looked at me, his eyes bloodshot from lack of sleep. "We're suing them. Every last one of them."

"Who exactly?"

"DiMarco. Trent. That whole UWA operation. All of them." He gestured at the papers spread across his desk. "Theft of intellectual property. And my belt! Plus, something called tortious interference. The works."

"Stan, what happened Saturday night?"

"I drove by to see how many cars were in the parking lot."

"I heard you caused a scene. Nearly got arrested."

Stan dismissed this with a wave of his hand. "I confronted a thief and a con man. DiMarco stole my champion and my belt. What was I supposed to do, send a fruit basket?"

"Maybe not threaten to shove his head up his own ass in front of a crowd?" I suggested.

"That little prick DiMarco had the nerve to act like he was doing me a favor, offering me a 'legends' spot on his shows."

I bit back a sigh. "Let me guess. You didn't take it well."

"I told him exactly what he could do with his 'legends' spot," Stan confirmed. "Then his rent-a-cops escorted me out. Power-tripping mall security rejects."

There was more to the story, I was certain, but getting an unvarnished version from Stan was impossible. He had an uncanny ability to cast himself as the babyface in every story, no matter the truth.

"So, what's your plan with these lawsuits?" I asked, nodding toward the papers.

"We file them tomorrow. Hit them hard and fast. DiMarco's got money, but he doesn't have the stomach for a legal battle. He'll fold."

I'd heard this particular strain of wishful thinking from Stan before. The last time he'd gone the legal route against a competing promotion, we'd spent six thousand dollars we didn't have on lawyer fees, only to drop the case when it became clear we had no actual grounds to sue.

"And Trent? You think he's going to be intimidated by legal threats?"

"That title belt alone is worth three grand. That's theft."

"Technically, we paid closer to $750—"

"Technically nothing! If it's over a certain amount, then he'll get prosecuted for grand larceny or something. The belt belongs to this promotion. End of story."

I decided to change tack. "What about Friday's show?"

"We should move to Saturdays."

"Why?"

"They want to go toe to toe with Stan the Man? I'll put my show up against their bullshit any day."

"Our guys did good in Chicago, by the way."

It worked. Changing the subject jarred him enough that he stopped ranting. "Oh. Right. Good. I'm glad they did well."

"That promoter would book through us again, but if we're not available on Saturdays . . ."

He looked down and then got a second wind. "Luke, I built this territory from nothing. And now some car dealer with daddy's money thinks he can just waltz in and take it all?" He shook his head. "Not happening. Not without a fight."

Looking at Stan in that moment—the bags under his eyes, the gray pallor of his skin—I had a hard time deciding what I felt. Frustration? Loyalty? Pity?

"We'll figure it out," I said, the words sounding hollow even to me.

"Oh, before I forget." He reached into his desk drawer and pulled out a folder. "Here's the bracket for the tournament."

I took the folder, glancing at the bracket inside. Eight names were scrawled in Stan's distinctive handwriting, arranged in a single-elimination format. Mike, the heel, was positioned for an easy path to the finals. Jim would face tougher competition. The other spots were filled with our remaining regulars including Bad Brad, Stew, and a name I was surprised to see. Joey.

At the bottom of the bracket, Stan had written in capital letters: WINNER GETS CROWNED CHAMPION.

"I'm not sure Joey will be ready in time," I said.

"He will be. He wouldn't miss this opportunity."

THIRTY-THREE

THE NEXT DAY, Joey walked in to training a few minutes late wearing pressed khakis and a button-down shirt that looked jarringly out of place. He carried a small folder under his arm.

"Well, look at you," I said. "How'd it go?"

Joey's face broke into a small, hesitant smile. "I got it. Benefits start after ninety days. Paid vacation. The whole deal."

"That's fantastic," I said, meaning it. "When do you start?"

"A month from Monday. As long as I pass the drug test—"

The door to Stan's office swung open, and The Man barreled out, clutching his coffee mug and a stack of papers. He stopped short when he saw Joey.

"What the hell are you dressed like that for? Sunday school?" Stan barked, eyeing Joey's outfit.

Joey shifted uncomfortably. "Just had some stuff to take care of today."

Stan grunted, unconvinced. He tossed his papers onto the folding table.

Joey glanced at me, a flicker of panic crossing his face. I gave him a small nod, silently promising to run interference if needed.

"I actually wanted to talk to you about something, Stan," Joey began.

Stan waved him off. "Later. First, did you see this shit?" He jabbed a finger at one of the papers he'd brought in—some kind of promotional flyer. "DiMarco's people are plastering these all over town."

He unfolded a glossy flyer that featured a stark black silhouette against a red background. The figure was of a wrestler, but with a question mark superimposed over the face. Below it, in bold text:

#WhosNextToDefect?

"Yeah, I saw. They were on all the cars at Heartland Products," Joey said, then quickly added, "I was passing by and noticed them."

Stan's face reddened as he crumpled the flyer. "Son of a bitch is trying to poach more of my talent." He paced the length of the makeshift ring, muttering curses. "First Trent, now this."

Mike was working with a couple of new trainees when he heard the commotion. "Hey, Luke," Mike called out, then noticed Stan's agitated state. "Everything okay?"

"DiMarco's playing mind games," I explained, gesturing to the crumpled flyer in Stan's hand. "Trying to stir up trouble."

Stew picked up one of the flyers from the table and studied it. "Kind of smart. Gets people talking, wondering who's gonna jump ship next."

Stan whirled around. "Nobody's jumping anywhere!" He paused for a second. "Enough about that motherfucker."

He strode to the desk and unfurled a large sheet of paper containing the tournament bracket with eight names. Mike hopped out of the ring to look. He was nonchalant about it, but checked where his name appeared. Stew and Eddie did the same.

"Joey," Stan said, "you're in too. First-round match against Bad Brad."

Joey froze. I could see the conflict play out on his face—the pull of opportunity against the practicality of his new job.

"Stan, I don't know if I'll be ready," he said carefully. "My shoulder is still—"

"You'll be ready," Stan interrupted, clapping him on the shoulder. "This is your shot, kid. The break you've been waiting for."

Joey's eyes pleaded for help. I stepped forward.

"Maybe we should consider the timing, Stan. Joey's recovery—"

"Will be complete by the show," Stan finished for me. "Right, Joey?"

Joey hesitated. "Yeah," he said finally. "I'll be ready."

Stan smiled triumphantly. "Damn right you will. This tournament is going to put us back on the map. DiMarco thinks he can steal our champion? Fine. We'll make a new one—a better one." He jabbed a finger at the bracket. "One of you is walking out with gold."

"You okay?" I asked Joey out of earshot of the others.

"I was going to tell him about the job," Joey whispered, his voice strained. "Now what do I do? That's right when I'm supposed to start at Heartland."

Before I could answer, Stan called out, "Joey! Get your gear on. It's time to get back in the ring. Your shoulder is fine, right?"

Joey's posture slumped slightly, then straightened with resignation. "Coming," he called back, then turned to me. "Rachel's going to kill me."

As Joey walked away to change, I caught sight of the crumpled UWA flyer on the floor. The question mark seemed to mock us all.

#WhosNextToDefect?

Maybe the better question was: who would want to stay?

Joey changed into his gear and joined the others in the ring. I hung back at my table, reviewing the tournament brackets and making notes. Mike stepped away from ringside to talk to me.

"So," he said, keeping his voice low, "heard you had an interesting night at the motel."

I froze, pen hovering over the paper. "What are you talking about?"

Mike's smirk widened. "Scarlett?" He leaned in. "The room at the end of the hall isn't as private as you thought."

I felt my neck get hot. "Nothing happened."

"Sure," Mike said, clearly not believing me. "That's why she was sneaking out of your room at 4 AM. For the continental breakfast, I assume?"

Before I could respond, Stew joined us, his massive frame casting a shadow over the table. "What are we whispering about?"

"Luke's motel adventure," Mike supplied helpfully.

"With the redhead?" Stew was giddy.

"Can we not do this right now?" I hissed, acutely aware that Stan could return at any moment. "I have shit to do."

Mike kept pushing. "How was she? Teach you a new hold?"

"I'm not discussing this," I said firmly.

"What's her finisher?" Stew asked. "That's important information. Tells you a lot about a person."

"It was nothing," I insisted. "Just a... moment. It doesn't mean anything."

Mike and Stew exchanged glances.

"Look," Mike said, his voice gentler, "nobody's judging. God knows we've all had road hookups. Just... be careful. Wrestling gets lonely. Easy to mistake convenience for connection."

"I don't need relationship advice from you two," I said, more sharply than I intended. But they weren't wrong about the loneliness.

Stew wasn't deterred. "Hey, some of us have it figured out." He lumbered to his feet, walking deliberately to the nearest ring post. With theatrical gravity, he wrapped his massive arms around it and planted a loud, wet kiss on the padded corner. "Wrestling's my wife. Never disappoints, always there when I need her, and doesn't care if I come home late smelling like other men."

I couldn't help but laugh. Several of the trainees paused their drills to stare at Stew's display.

"You're all insane," I said, shaking my head.

"Yep," Stew agreed cheerfully, giving the ring post one final pat. "But we're your kind of insane. That's why you stick around." He stared at the crumpled UWA flyer. "That's why we all do."

Mike nodded in agreement. "For what it's worth," he said, "it's good to see you acting like a human being for once. Even if it was just for a night."

Thirty-Four

I WAS SCROLLING through the promotion's email—mostly out of shape guys asking questions about training with us—when a message caught my eye. The subject line read: "Request from Pine Grove Adult Care Home."

My finger hovered over the delete button. Another request for free tickets probably. We got them all the time—charities, schools, youth groups. Stan's policy was simple: "If they can't pay, they can't play." But something made me open this one.

Dear Mr. Weizenschmidt,

My name is Elaine Mercer, and I work as a support coordinator at Pine Grove Adult Care Home. We provide residential care for adults with developmental disabilities. Several of our residents are passionate wrestling fans and a few of them have attended your shows with their families in the past. For many of them, your wrestlers are real-life superheroes.

One resident in particular, Danny (who's 34 but developmentally around 12), talks about Mike "The Bruiser" constantly and has collected every flyer we've been able to find featuring him.

I was wondering if it might be possible for our group (6 residents, 2 staff) to attend your upcoming show? Perhaps even meet some of the wrestlers briefly afterward? I understand completely if this isn't possible, but I wanted to reach out as it would mean the world to them.

Sincerely,

Elaine Mercer

Support Coordinator - Pine Grove Adult Care

I read it twice. Her timing couldn't have been worse. Ticket sales were abysmal. Half the roster was eyeing UWA. The last thing we needed was to give away eight tickets to a show that wasn't selling. Still, I found myself typing a reply.

Elaine,

Thanks for reaching out. We'd be happy to arrange something for your group at this Friday's show. Let me know what accommodations your residents might need, and we'll make it work.

Luke Anderson

Operations Manager

Stan Weizenschmidt Promotions

I hit send before I could reconsider, knowing Stan would give me hell when he found out. But right now, I didn't care.

Friday night arrived, and I'd managed to keep the Pine Grove group a secret from Stan right up until he saw the comp list. He just looked at me and shook his head.

The van was easy to spot in the parking lot—white with the facility's logo painted on the side, a stylized tree with branches forming a protective circle. I stood by the side entrance and waited.

When the van doors slid open, a woman emerged first—practical clothes, no-nonsense ponytail, the look of someone who cared about her work. Behind her came the residents, each moving at their own pace.

"Hi," she said. "I'm Elaine. Are you Luke?"

I shook her hand. "Yes ma'am. We're glad you're here."

The first resident was tall and lanky with thick glasses, and wore a hand-decorated t-shirt with "THE BRUISER" written in uneven marker strokes across the front. *Danny,* I thought. *Mike's biggest fan.* I learned later that he had been attending our shows for years before moving into Pine Grove. The staff collected our show flyers whenever they saw them so he could hang them in his room.

"Are we really going to meet the wrestlers?" he asked Elaine, his voice pitched high with excitement. "Really?"

"Yes, Danny," she assured him with practiced patience. "After the show."

The rest of the group emerged gradually. Elaine introduced them each to me. There was an older woman named Margaret who moved with halting steps but whose eyes were sharp and alert. Thomas, a heavyset man who didn't speak but hummed continuously was followed by Sophia, a young woman with close-cropped hair who bounced slightly on her toes. The last two—Daryl, a tall African-American man and Carl, a white-haired older man—stayed close to Carlos, the second staff member.

"Everyone," Elaine announced, "this is Luke. He's the one who made this happen tonight."

Danny's eyes widened. "Do you know The Bruiser?"

"I do," I said, smiling despite myself.

Danny's face lit up. "I love the Bruiser!" He made an enthusiastic gesture meant to mimic one of Mike's signature taunts.

I led them inside, finding the seats I'd reserved in the second row—close enough to see everything but away from the rowdier fans who might be drinking. Once they were settled in, I noticed Thomas, the man who hadn't spoken, watching the ring with intense focus. His humming had changed, matching the rhythm of the entrance music currently playing.

"I've never seen him this engaged," Carlos said. "Usually, he's in his own world."

"Hello Indiana!" Stan said from the mic. "Are you ready for some professional wrestling action?"

He waited while the crowd roared back at him.

"We've got an exciting line up for you tonight. You'll see The DOUBLE TROUBLE!" He waited for the crowd to cheer. Then he continued, "How about MIKE THE BRUISER ALVAREZ?" A cascade of boos. "He's here tonight. So is JIM THE HAMMER TANNER!" The crowd cheered, like Pavlovian dogs. They knew who was the babyface and who was the heel in each of these matches, but just in case there was someone new, this 'pep talk' as Stan called it made it quite clear. As the cheers died down, Stan paused dramatically.

"And I have one more big announcement to make." The people leaned in, getting very quiet. "Ladies and gentlemen, I wanted to tell you what's going on tonight, because I think we owe you the truth. Trent Howard decided to quit working here without any notice and without any respect for this ring, for me, or frankly, for you. And while I'm not here to give anyone free advertising, you might hear that he's working somewhere else in town."

A smattering of boos echoed through the arena. "I've been doing this longer than a lot of you have been alive. I've seen wrestling promotions come and go. I've seen fly-by-night opera-tions try to put me out of business, and I'm still standing right here in front of a record crowd tonight!"

I don't know what kind of record Stan was talking about—it certainly wasn't an attendance one—but the crowd cheered anyway. Stan paused and I could tell he was thinking about his next words.

"SWP . . . well . . .thanks to you guys—we are the first, the last, and the best. We'll outlive them all."

The crowd went absolutely crazy for this. Stan probably should have left it there. But his ego wouldn't let him.

"And Tony DiMarco, you no good son of a bitch, if you want a war with me and my boys—you got it." The crowd exploded. Not because of what Stan said, but how he said it.

He then formalized the announcement he'd made last week about the tournament at "Fahrenheit Fury," promising that a new undisputed champion would be crowned that night.

I couldn't help wondering if we'd have enough wrestlers left by then to fill the bracket.

Once the matches started, I looked out from behind the curtain. The show itself was nothing special by our standards—the usual mix of decent matches and filler, the same storylines we'd been running for months. But the Pine Grove group cheered, booed, and gasped as if they were watching magic and they didn't care at all how the illusion was performed.

Danny, in particular, seemed ecstatic. His eyes were wide behind his thick glasses, his hands moving excitedly when Mike made his entrance. Margaret, who'd been so quiet before, now shouted encouragement at the top of her lungs. Sophia bounced higher in her seat with each near fall.

During intermission, I checked on them. "Enjoying the show?" I asked Elaine.

"It's awesome!" Danny exclaimed.

After the final bell, I led the group backstage as promised. I'd arranged with Mike and a few others to meet them briefly, but I was nervous—wrestlers could be unpredictable, and not everyone had the patience for this kind of interaction.

But my worry was unfounded. Mike Alvarez, who'd been in the business for twenty years, who'd wrestled in Japan and Mexico, who'd had tryouts with WWE back in his prime, treated Danny like he was the most important fan he'd ever met.

"You're Danny?" Mike said, his eyes lighting up with recognition when I introduced them. "Luke told me you were coming tonight."

Danny stood frozen, mouth open in shock at first. Then he launched into an excited, somewhat jumbled explanation of Mike's finishing move while Mike listened, nodding seriously as he signed an 8x10 for him.

Around the room, similar scenes played out. Stew took a photo with Thomas while the man's humming got louder the more excited he felt. Amber listened while Sophia, who had barely spoken all night, was now animatedly describing her love for her cat. I saw Jessica—Scarlett—maintain her distance from Amber for the sake of kayfabe, but she was smiling.

She and I hadn't spoken, not really. We kept things professional and acted like nothing had ever happened. Mike and Stew both grinned at me when they saw her, but thankfully, they didn't make it awkward.

Stan, who I didn't expect to make time for the Pine Grove bunch, charmed both staff members Carlos and Elaine with his signature charisma and thanked them for coming to the show.

"This is the best day ever," Danny said as Mike handed him an official t-shirt to replace the homemade one he was wearing.

As they prepared to leave, Elaine approached me, her eyes bright.

"I can't thank you enough," she said. "This will be all they talk about for months. You have no idea what you've given them tonight."

But what she didn't know was what they gave me. Gave us.

As they gathered by the door, I noticed Thomas lingering behind the group, watching the ring one last time. His usual humming had grown quieter. When Carlos gently approached to guide him toward the exit, Thomas carefully took a leftover flyer from the ticket table advertising tonight's show, folded it precisely in half, and tucked it into his pocket.

"He must have really liked it," Carlos said to me as they left the building.

Stan approached as the van pulled away. "Good crowd tonight," he said.

"Yeah," I agreed, still watching the taillights disappear. "They were."

THIRTY-FIVE

After the show, Darlene worked the bar alone, keeping track of a dozen tabs while fielding food orders and deflecting the occasional drunk's attempt at flirtation.

The wrestlers had claimed our usual corner. I nursed a beer, half-listening to Mike and Stew argue about who was "better"—Ric Flair or Hulk Hogan. (Flair for his in-ring work, Hogan for his drawing power—but no one asked me.)

"Earth to Luke," Mike said, waving a chicken wing in my face. "You even listening to us?"

"Sorry," I said, taking a pull from my beer. "Just thinking about stuff."

"This tournament's gonna be brutal," Stew said. "Three matches in one night if you make it to the finals. My knees are hurting just thinking about it."

Mike snorted. "You'll be lucky to make it past the first round, old man."

While they resumed their friendly ribbing, I saw that Rachel and Joey had claimed a small table across the room. Joey was still nursing his shoulder, grimacing slightly whenever he moved wrong. Rachel noticed each wince, her hand instinctively moving to his arm. I could read her lips saying, "You okay?" every few minutes.

Joey caught me looking at them and waved me over. "Luke!" he called. I pulled up a chair. "So, did Trent really bring the belt back with a tire mark on it?"

"Yeah, Stan said he found it on the doorstep to the warehouse. Said it looked like someone had run it over with their car." What I didn't tell him was that I wasn't sure it was true. I wouldn't have been shocked if Stan had run over the belt himself just to have a story to tell.

"Damn, that sucks. I just don't understand the disrespect. You want to leave, fine, but that's too much." Joey took a gulp of his beer. "I'll be right back. Gotta piss."

Once he was gone, I asked Rachel, "How's he really doing?"

"His shoulder's hurting him more than he's letting on," she admitted. "He should be resting it."

"That's what I was afraid of. But now with this tournament—"

She interrupted me, glancing at the bathroom door. "He got the job, you know. At Heartland."

"I know. He told me."

"Good benefits. Steady pay. A real future." I was struck by the intensity in her eyes. "So I don't know why he's risking all that for another shot at playing wrestler."

Her words stung. Partly because of the dismissiveness, but mostly because I couldn't argue with her. Joey had a real opportunity. And here he was, risking it for one more chance at glory in a business that would almost certainly use him up.

"Wrestling's in his blood. Same as all of us."

"I know you care about him, Luke. At some point, don't you think—"

"He's a tough kid." Silence filled the space between us.

"I was Kole's nurse," she said, finally.

"What?"

"In the ER. I worked the night shift after WrestleBlast." Her eyes held mine, unflinching. "I saw the scans, Luke. He had a spinal contusion. Do you know what that means?"

"No."

"It means he was millimeters away from permanent paralysis," she continued. "If he'd landed just slightly differently, he might never have walked again."

"He's recovering, though," I said weakly. "Stan said—"

"I don't care what Stan said." There was no anger in her voice, just a steady, clinical certainty. "I've seen the damage, up close. I've watched patients come in with injuries like his, thinking they'll be back to normal in weeks. Some of them never fully . . ."

Before she could finish her statement, the door to the Wing Place swung open and a hush fell over our corner. Trent Howard stood in the doorway, surveying the room with a smirk. He looked different—new gear, new haircut, a new swagger. UWA's brand new shiny belt hung over his shoulder, the gold catching the dim bar lights.

"Well, look what crawled back," Mike growled, starting to rise from his seat.

Jim put a hand on his arm. "Don't."

Trent spotted our crew, and his smirk widened. He started across the room, a young woman trailing behind him. She wore an oversized UWA t-shirt and looked nervously around the bar.

"If it isn't Stan's loyal dogs," Trent called out, loud enough for the whole bar to hear. "How's it feel being on the sinking ship?"

Mike stood up. "Why don't you come find out?"

Conversations died as people turned to watch. Darlene looked up from behind the bar, her hand likely moving toward the baseball bat she kept under the counter.

"Easy, Mike," I said, standing up as well and walking back over to where the boys were sitting. "This isn't the time or place."

Trent laughed. "Listen to your babysitter, Mike. Wouldn't want to get hurt before your big tournament. Not that it matters —nobody's watching anyway."

That's when Joey appeared. His right arm hung awkwardly at his side. His left was clenched in a fist.

"You shouldn't be here," Joey said, his voice tight.

"It's a free country, rookie," Trent replied. "Besides, I'm just showing my girl a good time." The young woman beside him looked increasingly uncomfortable. "Letting her see how the other half lives before we head over to a real bar."

Rachel had moved to Joey's side, her hand on his good shoulder. I could see the fear in her eyes—not of Trent, but of what Joey might do.

"Joey," she said softly. "Let's just go."

Trent noticed the interaction and his eyes lit up with cruel amusement. "Listen to the bitch, Joey."

Joey lurched forward, but Rachel held him back. "He's not worth it," she whispered.

Trent laughed again, then turned to the young woman beside him. "Come on, Ashley." He shot one last look at us. "See you boys at the Armory. Oh wait—I'll be working a real show that night."

As he turned to leave, he bumped deliberately into Joey's bad shoulder. Joey winced, biting back a curse.

Mike lunged forward—but Trent was already moving toward the door, Ashley in tow. The girl glanced back once before following Trent. He was just past the bar when from his left, Stew grabbed him by the throat with one of his giant hands. He hoisted him off the floor a few inches.

"Don't you ever come back here." His calm intensity was chilling. "Do you understand?"

Trent gasped for air, but signaled that he did indeed understand. Stew released him and sat back down at his barstool, as if nothing had ever happened. Trent scurried for the door.

"Punk-ass bitch." Mike dropped back into his seat.

"We're heading out," Rachel said to no one in particular. I saw worry in her eyes, and something else—a silent plea for help, maybe. "Joey needs to rest that shoulder."

As they gathered their things, I walked over to them. "You want me to walk out with you? Just to make sure he's gone?"

"He's gone, Luke. Stew scared the shit out of him," Rachel reassured me.

"Yeah. Well, let me know how you're feeling tomorrow. You don't need to be in the ring if you're not 100%."

Joey's eyes were still on the door where Trent had exited.

I turned to Rachel quietly. "Please let him know that it's okay if he won't be ready to work the tournament."

"He doesn't want to have to choose." She searched my face. "You could help him with that, Luke."

Her words unsettled me.

"I'll see what I can do," I said finally.

"Thank you."

When I joined the wrestlers, Jim asked, "Did you see that girl with Trent? She looked scared to death."

Mike shook his head. "That shit's gonna catch up to him one day."

As the conversation moved on, I noticed Stew staring at his beer, fingers tapping lightly against the bottle.

"Stew," I said. He looked up. "You good?"

He held my gaze for half a second longer than usual.

"All good, Luke."

Darlene dropped off another round, patting my shoulder as she passed. "You boys doing okay?"

"Never better," I lied, reaching for my fresh beer.

Thirty-Six

Joey moved like a man twice his age.

I watched from my table as he attempted a simple lock-up with Stew, his face contorting in pain every time pressure was applied to his right side. The shoulder injury wasn't getting better —if anything, it seemed worse than it had been at the Wing Place on Friday.

"Loosen up, Joey," Stan called from across the warehouse, not even bothering to look up from the Sunday paper, which he always waited to read until Monday. "You're moving like my grandmother, and she's been dead fifteen years."

Joey nodded grimly and reset his position. Stew caught my eye over Joey's shoulder, his expression asking a silent question. I gave a subtle head shake. Don't push it.

Stew eased off, telegraphing his moves more obviously, giving Joey space to work. It was painful to watch. Joey was usually more fluid, smooth. Now his movements were mechanical, hesitant. Each bump drew a wince, each lock-up a grimace.

Mike sidled up next to me, arms folded across his chest. "Kid's hurting."

"Yeah."

"Tournament's in three weeks."

I didn't respond. We both knew the math. Joey's new job was set to start right after Fahrenheit Fury, our August event. His shoulder needed rest—weeks of it, not days. But Stan was pushing him to be ready, counting on him for the tournament.

"Did you hear?" Mike said.

I turned to him, surprised. "What?"

"The next defection? Eddie Evans."

"No shit?"

"DiMarco put him on their show. Main event against Trent." He kept his voice low, eyes flicking toward Stan. "Eddie was wearing UWA gear, new entrance music, whole nine yards."

"Shit." I ran a hand through my hair. Eddie the Extreme Evans wasn't a top draw, but he was reliable and had been with us for years.

"Stan know yet?"

Mike shook his head. "Don't think so. No one's had the balls to tell him."

In the ring, Joey attempted a shoulder block and immediately crumpled, his face ashen. Stew helped him to his feet, concern evident on his face.

"Alright, take a break," Mike called out.

Joey climbed out through the ropes. "I'm fine."

"Joey—"

"I said I'm fine."

"Yeah, well, it won't do you much good if you can't lift your arm above your head," I said. "Take the rest of training off."

Joey started to protest, but I cut him off. "That's not a suggestion."

As Joey climbed out of the ring, Stan looked up from his papers, frowning. "Where's he going?"

"He's done for today," Mike said.

Stan's frown deepened. "Tournament's coming up. He needs the reps."

"He needs to heal." I lowered my voice. "Look at him, Stan. He can barely raise his arm."

Stan looked at Joey, who was gathering his gear with one hand, the other hanging limply at his side. For a moment, I thought I saw concern on Stan's face.

"He'll be fine. He's tough."

"Yeah, but—"

"Speaking of the tournament," Stan said, changing the subject, "we need to talk about the bracket."

"What about it?"

"Eddie's out."

I blinked. "You know?"

"Course I know." Stan scoffed. "Think I don't keep tabs on DiMarco's shit? Good riddance."

His cavalier attitude didn't fool me but I knew better than to challenge him. "So, what now?"

"Motherfucker!" He turned the newspaper around to show me a giant UWA advertisement featuring Trent flexing. Stan crumpled the newspaper and threw it in the trash. "Alright, we're done for the day. Everyone out except Luke."

"I've got an idea," he said, looking up as I sat across the table from him. There was a manic gleam in his eyes. "I know exactly how we're gonna fix this."

"How?"

"Sy Reaper." Stan said it like I should be impressed. "Been tearing up the Detroit scene for years. Real hardcore—barbed wire, light tubes, the works."

"Sy 'The Soul' Reaper," I repeated slowly. "The guy who got

banned by three state athletic commissions for going too far with his hardcore shit?"

"That's him," Stan confirmed, looking pleased with himself. "I want to book him for Fury."

I pinched the bridge of my nose, feeling another headache forming. "Stan, we can't book that guy."

"He's a draw," Stan countered. "And he'll draw a crowd we don't normally get."

"Do we want that kind of crowd? Plus, he put a guy in the hospital last year," I said. "Stapled his forehead thirty-two times."

Stan waved this off. "That was a work. The guy was fine."

"And what about the thing in Cleveland? With the broken light tube?"

"Ancient history," Stan said. "Look, we need something to counter DiMarco's bullshit. Sy's a name. People will pay to see him."

He wasn't wrong. Sy Reaper had a reputation—the kind that made hardcore fans salivate and venue owners nervous. But I also couldn't forget the images I'd seen: Sy carving his opponent's forehead with a shard of broken glass, Sy wrapping barbed wire around his fist for "enhanced" punches, Sy tasing a guy's testicles with a stun gun.

"Who will he work with?"

"He'll bring someone in with him. Someone who doesn't mind getting carved up. Look, we need something besides this tournament. Something that will really get people talking."

I scanned the bracket that Stan had written out. Joey was in the first round with Bad Brad. Jim was supposed to square off with Eddie, and now there was a blank spot. Mike was facing Stew and rounding out the first round were two other blank spaces.

"Shouldn't we be focusing on the brackets? Figuring out the tournament?"

"I've got a plan for that. But... I take it you don't agree with me about bringing in Reaper?"

"It's just... Stan, we don't know this guy. He doesn't know us, our style—"

"I'll make sure he reins it in. It's a gimmick, Luke. It'll be fine."

"What will you tell him?" I asked flatly.

"You know. No knives, no excessive bleeding, no setting shit on fire." Stan gave a dismissive wave. "The usual."

The usual. I shook my head.

"What's his guarantee?" I asked instead.

"Two-fifty."

I whistled. That was well above our usual rate. "How much for trans?"

"Just a flat $250. No trans. He moves a lot of gimmicks and I'll let him keep all of that."

"Two-fifty is a lot, Stan."

"I know." Stan's face hardened. "But DiMarco's trying to run us out of business. And I'm not going out without a fight."

Thirty-Seven

"Quarter three projections look solid, but we need a strong push to hit our annual targets."

Three weeks later, Eric paced in front of the conference room whiteboard, gesturing at a graph that showed our department's performance against goals. "Which brings me to our next agenda item."

I tried to focus, but my mind was preoccupied with keeping Stan from driving us off the cliff before Fahrenheit Fury. I kept drifting back to Joey's injured shoulder. To Sy Reaper and his "props." To the tournament this weekend that still didn't have a finalized bracket.

"The all-hands retreat is Friday through Sunday," Eric continued, jolting me back to the present. "It's our chance to showcase our team's innovations directly to the C-suite."

Shit. I'd forgotten about the retreat entirely.

"As you all know, this is a mandatory event for all employees. There might be a few rooms left for any of you who want to stay overnight and haven't booked yet. Any questions?" Eric looked around the table.

I raised my hand, trying to keep it steady. "Eric, about the retreat—"

"All the details are in the email I sent," he interrupted. "Location, agenda, what to pack."

"Right, but I have a conflict this weekend," I said. "A prior commitment that I can't—"

Twenty pairs of eyes turned toward me.

"The retreat is mandatory." He held my gaze for a long moment before turning back to the room. "Now, moving on to our product roadmap..."

As the meeting wrapped up, people filed out of the conference room, chatting about project deadlines. I gathered my notes slowly, hoping to avoid further conversation, but Eric lingered by the door.

"Luke," he said as the last person left. "Look, I've been patient with your weekend wrestling thing. Your work gets done, you show up Monday through Friday, that's all I've cared about. But this retreat is different."

I said nothing. What could I say?

Eric sighed, his expression softening slightly. "We've had this conversation before. About commitment. About priorities. About potential advancement."

"I know."

"I think you have potential here. Real potential. But you keep holding yourself back with this... side project."

"It's not just a side project," I said.

Eric leaned against the table. "Then what is it? Because from where I stand, it looks like you're choosing to referee amateur wrestling matches over your professional future."

Refereeing amateur wrestling matches. Is that what he thought I did?

"People there depend on me," I said.

"And people here don't?" Eric's voice sharpened again. "The

entire executive team will be there this weekend. Attendance isn't optional."

"I understand that, but—"

"But nothing." Eric cut me off. "I need you to hear this clearly, Luke. The company is looking for any excuse to trim headcount. Do you understand?"

"I'll figure it out," I said finally.

Eric studied me for a long moment. "Good." He turned to leave, then paused at the door. "Silvertech needs to be your priority."

I pulled out my phone and saw three missed texts from Stan:

> Sy confirmed for Friday.

> Says he's bringing "special equipment." You handle that.

> Need you at venue early Friday. 4 pm sharp

I typed a response, deleted it, typed again.

> We need to talk.

Three dots appeared. Then Stan's reply:

> About the bracket?

I stared at the screen, feeling fifteen years of compromises, of choosing wrestling over everything else, of telling myself it was worth it.

> About everything.

Thirty-Eight

The Carrington Hotel's conference center hummed with energy. Men and women in business attire clustered around high-top tables, balancing coffee cups and notepads while exchanging corporate small talk. Phrases like "synergistic approach" and "scalable solutions" floated through the air, a language I'd never fully learned to speak.

Kayfabe, shoot, work, gimmick, heat, finish. That language I did know.

At 1:00 PM, I found myself in a workshop about server optimization. By 1:42 PM, I was getting panicked. If I left within the next eighteen minutes, I could make it to the Armory by 4 PM. And I'd miss all the Friday rush hour traffic. I ducked out of the room and headed for my car.

"Luke!"

I turned to see Eric approaching, flanked by a tall, silver-haired man I recognized as the company's CFO.

"Harold, this is Luke Anderson, one of our technical engineers," Eric said. "Luke, Harold Winters, Chief Financial Officer."

I shook the man's hand, forcing a smile. "Pleasure to meet you, sir."

"Eric tells me you've been spearheading our cloud migration," Harold said. "I'd love to hear more about the cost implications."

"Actually," Eric interjected before I could respond, "Luke's leading the technical demonstration tomorrow morning. He'll walk everyone through the migration architecture and expected ROI."

Tomorrow morning. I hadn't prepared any demonstration. Hadn't even known I was supposed to.

"Looking forward to it," Harold said, nodding approvingly before being pulled away by another executive.

As soon as he was out of earshot, I turned to Eric. "Technical demonstration?"

"It was in the itinerary I sent out three weeks ago," Eric said. His eyes communicated more than his words.

"I must have missed that," I said, feeling a cold sweat break out on the back of my neck.

"Apparently." Eric's tone was mild, but the message was clear. He could see right through me.

As he walked away, my mind raced. The demonstration tomorrow would require at least a few hours of preparation. Charts, slides, talking points—none of which I had ready. I'd intended to be back at the hotel by midnight, just enough time to crash and appear bleary-eyed but present at tomorrow's sessions.

My phone buzzed in my pocket. A text from Stan:

> Where are you? I need you.

> I'll be there by 4.

I saw our team's administrative assistant in the hallway. "Hey, Diane. Something's come up—family emergency. Would you mind telling Eric I had to step out? I'll be back as soon as possible."

She agreed without question, the magic words "family emergency" activating the automatic sympathy protocol. I felt a twinge of guilt for the deception, but not enough to stop me from walking toward the hotel lobby.

As I reached the parking lot, my phone buzzed again. Eric this time:

Where are you? Breakout starting.

My hand was on the car door. This was it—the point of no return. One more step and I'd be choosing wrestling over my career, exactly as Eric had warned against.

I got in the car and started the engine.

Sorry. Family emergency. Will explain later.

As I pulled out of the Carrington's parking lot, I caught sight of myself in the rearview mirror.

"You're an idiot," I told my reflection.

My reflection offered no argument.

I arrived at the Armory at 3:49 PM, having broken several speed limits en route. The parking lot was already filling up, fans in wrestling t-shirts milling around, waiting for doors to open at 7:00. I never understood why they got there so early, but every week there they were, standing out in the heat, the cold, and the rain.

My phone had been buzzing non-stop—texts from Stan, from Mike, asking if everything was okay.

Stan was waiting on me the moment I stepped through the back entrance.

"Where the hell have you been?" he demanded, his face flushed with anger or stress or both. "We've got a crisis."

"What happened?" I asked, shifting into troubleshooting mode.

"The Blade is out. Food poisoning or some bullshit." Stan ran a hand through his thinning hair. "We're down to seven for the tournament."

"Who'd you get to replace Eddie?"

"Kid named Tyler Blaze. Works the Toledo circuit. Green as grass, but he's here and he's cheap." Stan gestured to a young man with dyed-red hair who couldn't have been more than twenty-two.

"So, we've got seven. We can still make it work. First round: Joey versus Brad, one of the twins versus Stew, Jim versus this Tyler kid, and Mike gets a bye."

Stan shook his head. "The twins aren't coming tonight. Said they had a booking in Louisville."

"So, we're down to six." I sighed. "Alright, we can still make it work. Adjust the bracket to—"

"Already did," Stan cut in. "Joey versus Brad, Mike versus Stew, and Jim versus Tyler in the first round. And we'll just throw those two new kids in there and let Sy run in and beat the hell out of them. That can lead right into his match and will make Mike's bye still work."

It wasn't ideal, but it would work.

"Have you talked to Reaper?"

"Last night. He'll be here."

"Okay," I said, rubbing my temples. "Let me check in with everyone, make sure we're on the same page."

I made my rounds, confirming match details with each

wrestler. When I got to Joey, I said, "We're going all the way with you, you know?"

"Really?" He looked stunned.

"Yeah, but don't tell Stan I told you."

"But Luke. I don't want that."

Before I could respond, the back door banged open. Sy "The Soul" Reaper looked exactly like his photos: tall, gaunt, with long black hair and arms covered in scars and tattoos. Behind him followed a shorter, stockier man carrying two large duffel bags.

He shook everyone's hand. "Sy," he said, introducing himself to each of the boys.

"Luke," I said when shaking his hand. Softly. A wrestler's handshake.

"Who can we talk to about setting up some gimmicks?" Sy asked, his voice surprisingly soft for a man of his reputation.

Stan hurried over, all smiles and handshakes. "We've got a spot on the merch table just for you guys."

As they walked toward the far end of the backstage area, I caught sight of the duffel bags. One was partially unzipped, revealing the glint of barbed wire and what looked like a small staple gun.

THIRTY-NINE

The first round of the tournament went better than expected. Joey managed to work around his injury, keeping the action simple but effective. He and Brad put on a decent eight-minute match that ended with Joey scoring a clean pin after a dropkick and a small package.

Mike and Stew were next. Mike was calling the match—as the heel, he naturally took the lead—and had planned for Stew to make a comeback before cutting him off with a clothesline over the top rope.

"Comeback, ropes, clothesline, floor," he reminded Stew while they were resting in a headlock. Simple enough.

But when the moment came, Mike hit the ropes, rebounded with good speed, and caught Stew with a solid clothesline. Stew, all 400 plus pounds of him, went up and over the top rope as planned. But as he did, his right boot got tangled between the top and middle rope.

He was now suspended upside down on the outside of the ring, one leg caught in the ropes, arms dangling toward the floor. His face began turning red from the blood rushing to his head.

"Holy shit!" Joey was beside me at the curtain. "Did they mean to do that?"

"No." To Mike's credit, he played it like he'd deliberately trapped Stew in this humiliating position, though. He strutted around the ring, pointing and laughing at Stew's predicament—but really he was giving Stew and the referee time to free him.

"I'm stuck!" Stew hissed to the referee, low enough that only the front row might hear. "Can't get loose!"

The referee, trying to maintain kayfabe, leaned in as if checking on Stew's condition while actually attempting to help free his leg. But the ropes had twisted into a vice around Stew's calf, and his weight was only making it tighter.

"This is a fuckin' disaster," Stan growled, appearing beside me.

The crowd began to realize something was wrong as Stew's struggles grew more desperate. His face turned a deeper shade of purple. Smartphones started recording a viral moment in the making.

"Help him, dumbass!" a fan shouted at Mike, who was continuing his heel routine while shooting concerned glances at the referee.

"We need to do something," I said.

After what seemed like an eternity but was probably only thirty seconds, Stan decided. He pushed Tyler Blaze forward. "Get out there and attack Mike. Create a distraction while they get Stew untied."

"But I'm up next," Tyler protested. "Why would I—"

"Because I fucking said so!" Stan barked. "Go!"

Tyler sprinted down to the ring. The crowd's confusion was obvious as this rookie they didn't know slid into the ring and began attacking Mike, for no reason.

"This makes no sense," Joey said.

"Who fucking cares," Stan muttered. "Just send the second referee out to help get him down."

The other ref hurried through the curtain as the impromptu brawl continued in the ring. Mike made sure to keep the action as far from Stew as possible, taking the fight to the opposite side of the ring and eventually to the floor.

Meanwhile, both referees were now working frantically to free Stew's leg. They tried supporting his weight to release the pressure, but neither was strong enough to lift Stew's substantial bulk.

"Goddammit," Stan hissed, watching the monitor. "This is why Stew should have retired five years ago."

The ring announcer, seeing the referees struggling, set down his microphone and rushed over to help. Now three men were attempting to support Stew while untangling the ropes.

Finally, with the help of two trainees working security, they all managed to free his leg. Stew dropped heavily to the floor, landing awkwardly but rolling to all fours. The crowd, relieved, broke into spontaneous applause.

But Stew wasn't done. To everyone's surprise, he grabbed the ring apron and pulled himself up. With the borrowed time provided by Tyler's distraction, he rolled under the bottom rope and back into the ring.

"What the hell is he doing?" Stan demanded.

We watched in disbelief as Stew staggered to his feet, his face still red, a nasty rope burn visible on his calf. He limped to the edge of the ring where Mike was brawling with Tyler. Quietly, Mike told Tyler to throw him back into the ring.

"They're finishing the match," Joey said with respect.

Sure enough, as Mike got to his feet, Stew hit him with a surprisingly agile clothesline, then followed up with one of his signature moves—a running body splash in the corner. The crowd, initially confused by the booking chaos, rallied behind Stew's gutsy performance.

But Mike moved just in time and went behind Stew and

caught him in a schoolboy rollup. The referee, back in position, counted the pinfall.

Mike's hand was raised in victory and he jumped out of the ring quickly. Stew sat on the mat and sold his leg—though I'm not sure how much was him selling and how much it really hurt. Tyler had already come back through the curtain, shaking his head.

When Stew limped through the curtain moments later, his face was a mixture of pain, embarrassment, and professional pride.

"Jesus, Stew," Stan said, "What the hell happened out there?"

"My leg got caught," Stew panted, leaning against the wall.

"Fuck," Stan said.

"You OK, Stew?" I asked. "That looked really painful."

"The show must go on," Stew replied simply, wincing as he examined the deep rope burn on his calf. Joey handed him a water bottle.

"Why did you send the new kid out there?" Stew asked me.

"Stan told him to go," I shrugged. "He was in the wrong place at the right time. Seriously, are you OK?"

"Been better," Stew admitted. "Been worse too."

"Let's get some ice on that leg," I said as I helped steady him into a nearby chair. "At least you finished the match."

"What else was I going to do?" Stew asked, confused. "Leave everyone hanging?"

I laughed and he realized what he said. "Don't you dare tell that one to the boys," Stew warned, though his eyes crinkled with amusement. "I'll never hear the end of it."

Mike walked over with his phone out. Someone had already posted a video. Stew's dangling predicament was now on YouTube.

"Great," Stew turned red at sight of the video. "My legacy is complete. Stewie the Starmaker, the Nutcracker himself, and now the Hangman."

"Could be worse," I offered.

"How?"

"You could have ripped your tights again."

FORTY

Jim and Tyler were next. It was an uneven match, but it served its purpose. Jim did his best to guide the kid, but there were several obvious miscommunications. At one point, Tyler whiffed on a clothesline, missing Jim by a good six inches.

The crowd noticed, a few laughs and groans emerging from the front rows. But Jim, veteran that he was, adjusted and did the best he could to get back on track. Finally, Jim told the kid to go home. They went into the finishing sequence, which Tyler also screwed up. Finally, Jim pinned him with a small package.

"Sorry about that," he said as he passed me. "Kid was going too fast. I know we went home too soon."

I patted his shoulder. "Naw, we needed to cut time anyway thanks to Stew and Mike going long. But Joey won with a small package earlier, so we repeated the finish."

"Oh, damn. Sorry, Luke."

Next up was the match I was most worried about. Two green rookies, being thrown into the mix. Thankfully, they wouldn't have time to do too much before Sy Reaper's music hit.

"Are these kids ready for this?" Jim asked.

"I doubt it."

The two rookies, Doug Devine and Tex Hamilton, were new trainees who'd had maybe five matches between them. Stan had rushed them onto the roster, partially worried they'd be the next to defect. I'm not sure if they knew what they were in for, but they seemed thrilled just to be on the card.

The bell rang, and they locked up in an awkward collar-and-elbow tie-up that looked more like a middle school dance than professional wrestling. The crowd, still energized from the tournament matches, began to deflate visibly.

"This is terrible," Stan groaned beside me. "Give it thirty more seconds, then tell Chuck to play Reaper's music."

The rookies exchanged some basic moves–a headlock, an arm drag, a missed dropkick. Just as the crowd started a lackluster "Bor-ing!" chant, I signaled to Chuck and the lights cut out.

A distorted scream echoed through the speakers, followed by the grinding industrial metal of Sy Reaper's entrance theme. The crowd collectively inhaled, knowing something was about to happen but not quite sure what.

When the lights came back on, Sy stood in the ring, dressed in black leather adorned with metal spikes, his face painted in a grotesque skull design. In one hand, he held a barbed wire-wrapped baseball bat. In the other, a staple gun.

"Jesus Christ," I heard Jim mutter. "Is that thing loaded?"

The rookies in the ring looked confused, but their expressions were all part of the show. Before they could react, Sy attacked them both.

What followed was pure destruction.

Sy swung the bat, and Doug instinctively ducked. Then Sy

caught him with a stiff knee to the stomach that doubled him over for real. Tex tried to intervene, only to receive a forearm smash that sent him sprawling.

For the next three minutes, Sy dismantled both rookies with increasingly violent moves. He body-slammed Doug onto the barbed wire bat, which had been gimmicked to look worse than it was. He applied a chokehold to Tex that had the referee frantically checking if the kid was conscious. He pulled a bag of thumbtacks from his boot and scattered them in the corner, though mercifully Tex avoided having to bump into the pile.

The audience's reaction was split. Half were on their feet, cheering the chaos with chants of "Holy shit!" The other half sat in uncomfortable silence, parents covering the eyes of younger children.

Just when it seemed Sy might kill one of the rookies, his own entrance music hit again. Through the curtain emerged his scheduled opponent—"Mayhem" Max McKenzie, a heavyset, bearded man in tattered jeans and a flannel vest. He carried a garbage can full of weapons.

Doug and Tex, seeing their opportunity, rolled out of the ring and stumbled back up the ramp, nursing very real bruises and welts.

In the ring, Sy and Mayhem Max got to work. The garbage can was upended, spilling kendo sticks, a frying pan, a fluorescent light tube, and what appeared to be a mouse trap onto the mat.

"Who's gonna clean this shit up?" I asked Stan.

"Probably you," he replied, smiling.

"Hardcore garbage!" Jim had been watching at the curtain. "This is not wrestling, Stan. It's a circus act."

Stan didn't say anything but his smile had faded.

What followed was fifteen minutes of choreographed brutality. Sy took a kendo stick to the back, the crack echoing through the hall as welts rose visibly on his skin. Mayhem Max was stapled in the forehead, tiny droplets of real blood forming around the metal.

They brawled into the crowd, sending fans scattering as they exchanged weapon shots near the concession stand. Sy was slammed onto the merchandise table, which collapsed beneath him in a shower of his own t-shirts and DVDs. Mayhem Max took a backdrop onto the concrete floor that made the entire building shake.

By the time they made it back to the ring, I noticed several families with younger children gathering their belongings and heading for the exits. An older couple who had been regulars for years sat with arms crossed, visible disapproval on their faces.

"We're losing people," I said to Stan.

"Those guys love it!" he countered, nodding toward a group of men in their twenties chanting "One more time!" as Sy wrapped barbed wire around his fist.

The finishing sequence involved Sy climbing the turnbuckle with Mayhem Max laid out on a table at ringside. Sy launched himself from the top rope, crashing through both Max and the table in a sickening impact that had to have hurt them both for real. Sy threw Max into the ring, and the referee counted three as Sy draped an arm over his opponent's chest.

As Sy raised his arms in victory, streaked with sweat and blood, I caught sight of another angry father and his young son fleeing toward the exit. The boy was in tears.

The ring announcer said, "Ladies and gentlemen, we'll take a short intermission to clear the ring, and then it's time for the second half of the championship match of our tournament!"

Forty-One

My watch said 9:12 PM. The second half of the show would take at least an hour, maybe longer. Then I had a two-hour drive back to Indianapolis, and somehow, I needed to prepare for a presentation before 8 AM.

But those were problems for future Luke. Right now, I had a ring covered in thumbtacks and barbed wire to clean up.

"Let's get this ring cleared," I called to the crew.

As the trainees worked to move the debris, I walked back into the locker room. I saw that Sy had pulled up a chair near Joey. He was methodically removing his makeup with baby wipes. Without the skull face paint and manic energy, he looked almost ordinary—just a tired middle-aged man covered in scars.

"Everything good?" he asked.

I lied. "Yeah! It was great. Thank you so much."

He dabbed at a small cut on his forehead. "Thanks, man."

I stepped back and saw the two of them—a grizzled, scarred-up journeyman and then young Joey, full of potential and hope for a life that didn't result in permanent damage to his body. I wanted to tell him it wasn't worth it, that no championship—

especially one in Elmwood, Indiana—was worth derailing his future.

But who was I to give that advice? I'd just abandoned a career-critical retreat to be here.

"Are you sure you're good?"

Joey was firm. "I can do this, Luke."

"Just... be careful."

"Jim has a plan. We're gonna work my shoulder injury into the match. Might as well use what's real."

The semifinal match highlighted both Joey's skill and pain tolerance. Even with his injury, he and Jim had the best technical match of the rookie's young career. They worked a classic babyface versus babyface match, with Joey playing the resilient underdog against Jim's methodical, relentless offense.

Eight minutes in, Joey was visibly struggling, his face pale with pain each time his shoulder was involved in a move. But the crowd was fully invested, with chants of "Joey! Joey!" to encourage their new hero.

The finish came when Jim went to the top-rope for his elbow drop and Joey countered with a well-timed hurricanrana. Joey smoothly grabbed Jim's leg and held him down for the three-count. Joey would advance to the finals.

"You need to ice that shoulder. Now," Jim told him when they got backstage.

"I'm fine," he gasped, clutching his arm.

The ring announcer made a big show of Mike not having an

opponent in this round. Mike even went out and cut a promo on Joey that left the crowd ready to riot.

We needed to give Joey another minute or two to rest, so Stan went to the ring to announce the raffle winner. He pulled out the winning ticket, which unsurprisingly belonged to Lois, one of our loyal fans who seemingly always won the 50/50 split the pot because she bought multiple arm's lengths of tickets.

"Ladies and gentlemen," Stan's voice boomed through the hall, "tonight's audience is one of the best we've ever had! And it's because we've got the best fans in the entire world! It's because of you that we've been in business this long–and it's because of you that we're gonna keep rocking and rolling until I take my last breath. They'll have to kill me to stop me from producing the best damn wrestling show in the Midwest!"

The crowd cheered, but it was clear they were tired.

The ring announcer took the mic back and said, "Ladies and Gentlemen, it's now time for the MAIN EVENT! This is the championship match of the Fahrenheit Fury Championship Tournament! The winner will be the NEW Undisputed SWP Heavyweight Champion!"

Joey entered through the curtain. Usually, the heel would come out first, but Mike had pitched an idea. So, I told Chuck to switch up the order of entrance music.

Once Joey was halfway down the aisle, Mike didn't wait to be introduced but came barreling through the curtain and attacked Joey in the aisle. He threw him into the ring.

Joey had won the crowd over with two gutsy matches on a bad shoulder, while Mike had waltzed into the finals without breaking a sweat. The crowd hadn't forgotten that—and when Mike came barreling through the curtain before the bell, they lost their minds.

Over the next few minutes, Joey would mount a comeback, only for Mike to target the injured shoulder. Joey would adapt, finding ways to attack without using his right arm, only for Mike to eventually regain control.

Ten minutes in, the crowd was fully invested, cheering Joey's hope spots and booing Mike's ruthless shoulder attacks. Even the smartest fans in the audience—the ones who knew it was all predetermined—were caught up in the drama.

The finish, when it came, was perfect. Mike, confident in his advantage, went for a leg drop. Joey moved at the last second, causing Mike to crash and burn. Both men got to their feet and with his last reserves of energy, Joey hit the ropes, Mike ducked, and Joey executed a picture-perfect sunset flip for the pin.

The hall erupted. Fans leaped to their feet, their roars nearly drowning out the music. Joey collapsed to his knees in the center of the ring.

Stan entered the ring, the battered championship belt in hand. He raised Joey's arm—the good one—and presented him with the title. Joey held it high, wincing through the pain, soaking in the adulation of the crowd. I had a lump in my throat.

As Joey celebrated, I checked my watch. 10:18 PM. If I left now, drove like hell, I might make it back to the retreat by midnight. Maybe I could salvage my tech career. Maybe Eric would understand.

Joey was now hugging Rachel, who was in the front row next to her father. Fans were congratulating him as he slowly made his way to the back.

My phone buzzed. A text from Eric:

> Hope the family is OK. Wondering about the presentation tomorrow. I need you.

> I'll be ready.

I grabbed my jacket and car keys, giving Stan a quick nod to indicate I was leaving. He frowned but didn't try to stop me.

Forty-Two

The Oakwood Room of the Carrington Hotel was packed by 8:07 AM, with executives and department heads nursing expensive coffee and making small talk. The air conditioning blasted with efficiency, leaving the room several degrees too cold for my comfort. My exhausted body interpreted this as a personal attack.

"You good to go?" Eric asked. "Harold's particularly interested in your ROI projections."

"Great," I said, hoping my voice sounded steadier than I felt. "Looking forward to sharing those."

I had no ROI projections.

What I had were cobbled-together slides copied from our last quarterly review, a vague understanding of cloud infrastructure, and approximately ninety minutes of sleep seized between 3 and 5 AM.

Eric lingered for a moment. "Everything okay at home?" His emphasis on "home" made it clear he knew exactly where I'd been.

"Family emergency resolved," I said, the lie sour in my mouth. "Thanks for asking."

He seemed unconvinced. "Good luck up there." The way he said it made it sound like a funeral rite.

Harold Winters entered the room, his silver hair immaculate above designer glasses that probably cost more than my monthly rent. Several VPs followed in his wake, their attention divided between their phones and Harold's anecdote about his recent golf game.

"Looks like we're starting," Eric said, moving to direct the executives to their seats. "You ready?"

"Born ready," I replied, a phrase I'd picked up from too many pre-show conversations with Stan. Eric's face did not look convinced.

The slideshow opened, revealing my hastily assembled Power-point. Twenty-three slides of recycled content, generic stock photos, and technical jargon that I hoped would mask the complete absence of original analysis. The title slide stared back at me: "Cloud Migration Architecture & ROI Analysis." Below it, my name and last quarter's date.

I hadn't even updated the date.

"Good morning, everyone," I began, my voice a half-octave higher than normal. "Today we're looking at the cloud migration architecture we've implemented and the projected return on investment."

The room settled into attentive silence as I clicked to the first slide.

It was a detailed technical diagram from last quarter's infrastructure assessment—one that had nothing to do with cloud migration. I stared at it for a moment too long, my sleep-deprived brain struggling to pivot.

"This is, uh, our current infrastructure," I improvised. "Before we discuss the migration, it's important to understand what we're starting with."

Harold leaned forward, squinting at the diagram. "I thought

we'd already transferred the CRM database to cloud servers last quarter. This shows it still on-prem."

A cold sweat broke out across my shoulders. He was right. The diagram was outdated—something I would have known if I'd spent more than ten minutes assembling this presentation.

"That's right," I said, channeling my inner Stan, who could sell anything with enough confidence. "This diagram is actually from Q2, which serves as our baseline for measuring progress."

I clicked to the next slide—a generic bar graph comparing costs with no specifics or labels.

"As you can see..." I began, then froze. I had no idea what this graph was supposed to show. It could have been server costs, maintenance hours, or the lunch preferences of the IT department.

"What exactly are we looking at here?" asked a VP whose name I should have known but couldn't recall. "Are these monthly or quarterly figures?"

Eric's face looked like he was mentally updating both of our resumes.

"These are... projected savings," I said, searching the unlabeled axes for any clue. "Quarterly, over the next fiscal year."

"But there are only three bars," Harold pointed out.

The room seemed to constrict around me. I blinked hard, trying to force my foggy brain to cooperate.

"Yeah, I see that," I said, the bullshit flowing freely now. "Looks like a graphical error. I'll get you the correct data later?"

For twenty excruciating minutes, I invented technical issues that didn't exist, solutions we'd never implemented, and cost savings pulled from thin air.

By the time I reached the "Questions?" slide—mercifully, the last one—the room had shifted from interested engagement to uncomfortable pity. Harold was checking his watch. Two VPs scrolled through emails. Eric sat with his arms crossed, eyes fixed on the table in front of him.

"So, to summarize," I said, fighting to keep my voice even, "our cloud migration strategy provides robust scalability, significant cost savings, and improved security posture. I'd be happy to answer any questions."

The silence was deafening.

Finally, Harold cleared his throat. "I appreciate the overview, Luke. I was hoping for more concrete figures on the ROI timeline, but perhaps we can follow up separately."

It was the corporate equivalent of a pat on the head—a dismissal so gentle it somehow hurt more than outright criticism.

"Of course," I said. "I can provide more detailed projections after the session."

Harold nodded, already turning to Eric. "Let's move on to the next item on the agenda."

I gathered my notes, aware of eyes carefully avoiding mine as I made my way back to my seat. Eric just stared at me before standing to introduce the next presenter.

I slumped in my chair, exhausted and humiliated. My phone buzzed in my pocket—likely Stan with some new crisis, some logistical nightmare that needed immediate attention.

For the next hour, I sat in a fog, nodding at appropriate intervals as another manager presented a flawless analysis of market penetration strategies, complete with actual data and coherent conclusions.

When they finally called a fifteen-minute break, I made my way toward the exit, desperate for caffeine and a moment's escape from the stifling embarrassment of the room.

"Luke." Eric's voice stopped me at the door. "Got a minute?"

I followed him to a quiet corner away from the executives. We stood in silence, the consequence of my failure hanging between us.

"I won't ask where you really were yesterday," Eric began, his voice low. "I think we both know."

I said nothing. There was nothing to say.

"That presentation," he continued, "was the worst I've seen in fifteen years of management. Outdated data, no coherent structure, and you seemed completely unprepared."

"I know," I admitted. "I'll fix it. I can redo the whole analysis and—"

"No." The word was final, cutting me off. "You won't. I've given the tasks to someone else. So they'll get done right."

I could feel my career at Silvertech crumbling beneath my feet.

"I've spent two years advocating for you, Luke. Defending your split focus. Arguing for your advancement despite your... extracurricular commitments." Eric's fingers drummed briefly on the desk. "I did that because you're genuinely talented. But talent means nothing without commitment."

"I'm committed," I said, the protest weak even to my own ears.

"No, you're not." Eric's voice was tired rather than angry. "Not to Silvertech, anyway. I was pushing for you to get promoted. I really was. But after this? I can't."

I'd expected this, but the reality still stung. "I understand."

"Do you?" Eric leaned forward. "This is very serious."

My stomach dropped. "Are you firing me?"

"Not today." He rubbed his temples. "But I am putting you on a performance improvement plan effective Monday. Ninety days to demonstrate full commitment to your role here. No more disappearing acts, no more divided attention."

The implications were clear: choose Silvertech or choose wrestling.

"I need a response, Luke."

What could I say? That I'd spent fifteen years prioritizing a small-time wrestling promotion over everything else in my life? That I didn't know who I was without it? That the thought of walking away from Stan and the boys felt like contemplating voluntary amputation?

"I understand," I said finally. "I'll make it work."

Eric studied me for a long moment. "The executives' break runs another five minutes. Get yourself together before you come back."

He stood, closing his laptop with a decisive click. At the door, he paused. "You know what the saddest part is? You could be extraordinary at this job if you gave it even half the dedication you give to that wrestling... thing."

My phone buzzed again. This time I checked it.

Where are you??? We need to talk about last night's gate. UWA did 500+ paid last weekend. We're in trouble.

Forty-Three

I was twelve minutes late to training on Monday night. Not because of traffic or an emergency, but because Eric had scheduled a "check-in" meeting at 4:30 PM sharp—a not-so-subtle reminder of my new performance improvement plan. He'd spent forty minutes reviewing expectations, metrics, and the detailed documentation that would follow my every professional move for the next ninety days.

The warehouse lights were already on when I pulled into the gravel lot. Rachel's Honda was parked near the entrance. Through the windshield, I could see her sitting in the driver's seat, scrolling through her phone.

Inside, Joey sat on a folding chair near the ring, championship belt resting across his lap, not dressed for training. Stan paced nearby, shooting suspicious glances in Joey's direction. The other wrestlers were warming up half-heartedly, sensing something was off.

"Finally." Stan was in his usual mood. "Maybe now we can get started."

Joey looked at me, clearly having waited for my arrival before saying whatever he needed to say. He took a deep breath. "Can I talk to you guys for a minute?"

"Sure, Joey," I said.

"What's going on?" Stan asked.

"I went to the doctor this morning," he said, addressing both of us but looking at me. "My shoulder—if I keep wrestling, I'll need surgery eventually. And even with surgery, there could be permanent damage."

Stan's face went still. Not angry, not argumentative—just blank, as if someone had switched him off.

Joey continued into the silence. "I know the right thing to do would be to drop the belt in the middle of the ring and I want to do that, but the doctor said I wasn't allowed. Said it was too risky."

Stan didn't respond. He simply stared at Joey for a long, uncomfortable moment, then turned and walked away—straight to his office without a single word. He slammed the door.

Joey looked at me, not sure what to do. I put my hand on his good shoulder.

He looked at me. "My new job starts Wednesday. Benefits, retirement plan, the works. Rachel's cousin really came through." He looked down at the championship belt, his fingers tracing the metal plates. "I wanted to come tonight personally. To thank everyone."

He looked toward Stan's office.

"He just needs time," I said, hoping it was true. But Stan's silence was worse than any tantrum.

Mike approached, having overheard. "You're making the right call, kid. That job's a good opportunity."

"Thanks," Joey said. "I didn't want to just disappear. Not after everything."

One by one, the other wrestlers came over. Stew gave him a careful hug, mindful of his injury. "You're always welcome at the Wing Place on Fridays."

"Count on it," Joey replied with a small smile.

After the goodbyes, Joey handed me the belt. "What happens now?"

"We figure it out," I said. "We always do."

He motioned toward Stan's office. "Should I try to talk to him?"

"Better not," I said. "I'll handle it."

I walked him to the door. Outside, Rachel straightened in the driver's seat.

"I'm sorry, Luke," Joey said.

"You don't need to be. And don't worry. I've dealt with Stan for fifteen years," I assured him. "This is just another Monday."

Joey gave me a one-armed hug. "Thanks for everything. I mean it."

He climbed into the passenger seat. Rachel reached over and squeezed his hand.

When I walked back inside, the wrestlers had resumed their training, though the atmosphere remained subdued. I set the championship belt on the table and knocked on Stan's door.

"What?"

I opened the door. He was sitting behind his desk, staring at nothing in particular, his face unnervingly blank.

"Stan," I began, closing the door behind me.

"Two days," he said, his voice frighteningly calm. "Two full fucking days as champion. We built the whole damn promotion around him, and he walks away after forty-eight goddamn hours."

I remained silent.

"I saw something in him," Stan continued. "I stuck my neck out, put the belt on him over guys with twice his experience." His hand tightened into a fist on the desk. "And this is how he repays me."

"His shoulder—"

"Don't." Stan's eyes snapped to mine, the calm façade cracking. "Don't you dare defend him."

"He's making the right decision," I said carefully. "The doctor—"

"Fuck the doctor!" Stan was on his feet now, color flooding his face. He slammed his palm against the desk, making the computer keyboard jump. "You think Harley Race gave a shit what doctors said? Did Terry Funk retire when his knees gave out? This business is about sacrifice!"

I bit my tongue, letting him vent. This was the Stan I knew—all bluster and wounded ego.

"And you," he continued, jabbing a finger at me. "Standing there like his goddamn lawyer. 'He's making a responsible decision.' Since when do you take his side over mine?"

"I'm not taking sides," I said, maintaining my calm. "I'm saying he made the choice that's right for him."

Stan moved around the desk, his shoulders tensed as if ready for a physical confrontation. "The choice that's right for—" Stan cut himself off with a bitter laugh. "Listen to yourself. You sound like his mother or that dumb bitch he's fucking."

"Stan . . ." I held my ground as he drew closer.

"She's the one filling his head with this 'responsible decision' bullshit. She's the reason our new champion just walked out the door! Guys always quit over a piece of ass!"

"Stop," I said, feeling my patience thinning.

Stan went very still, inches from me now. His breath was coming in short, angry bursts. "You respect him for quitting?"

"I respect him for choosing. This business would chew him up and spit him out without a second thought."

"Is that what you think I do?" Stan's voice dropped to a dangerous quiet. "Chew people up and spit them out?"

"Sometimes, yeah. I do."

Stan leaned in, his eyes narrowing. "You ungrateful son of a bitch. I made you. Before me, you were nothing but some computer nerd with no life and no purpose. I gave you a place in this business."

I said nothing.

"Oh, now you got nothing to say? That sounds right. At least Joey has talent. What do you have? The ability to update a website? To fetch coffee? You couldn't hack it as a wrestler so you—?"

"That's enough," I said.

"No, it's not enough," Stan snarled. He paced back toward his desk, then whirled around. "Not by a long shot. You think you're indispensable? You're just another parasite living off my business! My vision!"

"Your vision is killing this promotion! Trent was your vision. Sy Reaper was your vision. And now we're bleeding talent and can barely make payroll!"

"So now it's my fault? It's you who can't keep these soft, entitled kids in line?"

"I'm not their Dad."

"They're cowards!" Stan shouted. His face reddened, a vein pulsing in his forehead as he kicked his chair aside. "Just like you've always been. Too afraid to get in the ring yourself. Instead, you hide behind your clipboard—"

For fifteen years, I'd absorbed Stan's anger, his insults, his manipulations. I'd justified it, excused it, compartmentalized it.

"Go fuck yourself, Stan," I said, the words emerging calm and clear.

Stan blinked in shock. "What did you just say to me?"

"You heard me." I walked toward the door. Then, I turned around and looked him in the eye. "Go fuck yourself."

"Don't you dare walk out that door," Stan threatened. "You walk out now, you're done here."

I opened the door and walked out.

Outside, the night air was cool against my face, a welcome contrast to the stifling atmosphere inside. Once in my car, I gripped the steering wheel and peeled away, waiting for the surge of guilt and responsibility to hit me.

It didn't come.

I turned onto the main road and kept driving, my phone lighting up with incoming calls from Stan that, for the first time in fifteen years, I had no intention of answering.

Forty-Four

Forty-eight hours later, I was back at training. Stan had texted and called repeatedly the first day and I left him on read. But eventually I listened to his voicemails. He sounded sincere enough and told me that he knew he couldn't run this promotion without me, so I relented and returned.

He'd also cooled off about Joey. He had me reach out to him and ask him to come to the show to formally announce his retirement and forfeit the title in person. That way, the fans could get some closure—and it wouldn't seem like another Trent situation. It was also his way of making sure that Joey wasn't secretly planning to defect to the UWA.

Stan greeted me with an awkward grin when I walked into the warehouse on Wednesday evening, neither of us acknowledging the things we'd said. The boys seemed relieved, as if their parents had called off a divorce at the last minute. Mike gave me a questioning look, but I just shrugged.

"So, did you call Joey?" Stan asked, his voice neutral.

"Yeah. He's good with it. This Friday works for him."

"Good, good. We'll do it before the main event. Make it

special." He was in promoter mode, calculating how to spin Joey's departure into a sellable moment. "We'll introduce the eight-man THUNDERdome cage match for the vacant title while he's there. And maybe we'll let Mike get some heat on Joey, too. Might as well take advantage of things."

I didn't argue, but there was no way Joey was doing anything physical. And Mike wouldn't do it unless Joey was on board. This time, Stan would not get his way; he had no power over Joey anymore. Joey had escaped what had trapped me for fifteen years. I envied him.

The door to the warehouse opened. A new face, a barely eighteen-year-old boy, held cash in his hand and a smile on his face. "I want to learn how to wrestle."

I looked at Stan. "Welcome aboard, kid. What's your name?" he said.

I shook my head. We were likely going out of business but that didn't stop Stan from taking this kid's money.

He had Mike get him started, with the basic bumps followed by the ritual of learning to run the ropes. The new kid grimaced as he peeled his shirt away from his skin, revealing the angry red welts beneath his arms where the ropes had punished his inexperience.

"Burns like hell, doesn't it?" Mike said.

"When does it stop?"

"It doesn't," Mike answered. "You just build up calluses until you can't feel it anymore."

Mike pulled his own shirt aside to reveal the thick, ridged skin under his arms—years of scar tissue built up like armor.

"That's wrestling," he said with a shrug. "It hurts until it doesn't."

FORTY-FIVE

Friday's show drew one hundred and twelve paid, our lowest attendance in years. The crowd was noticeably subdued, with empty chairs scattered throughout the Armory. Joey's retirement ceremony went smoothly—he gave a heartfelt speech about what wrestling and the fans had meant to him, laid the belt in the center of the ring, and shook hands with the boys on his way out. The fans gave him a decent reaction, but their applause felt perfunctory.

As Joey made his exit, he didn't look back at the ring. There was a certainty in his stride. When he passed me, he just nodded.

"Thirty? That's barely enough to cover my dinner?" Stew stared at the envelope in his massive hand, disappointment evident on his face. We were in the Wing Place after the show. "I usually get fifty."

"Attendance is down," I muttered. We all knew the reason. "Stan's doing what he can."

"UWA's paying guys a hundred for the same spot," Mike said quietly, nursing his beer. I hadn't heard for sure—the exact figure DiMarco was offering.

We sat in silence. Mike, Stew, Brad, Jim — veterans who had been with Stan for years. The question nobody wanted to ask: how long could this go on?

"Well, I'm not going anywhere," Jim declared, though no one had suggested he might. "I've been with Stan since the beginning. I'll go down with this ship."

Murmurs of agreement followed, but they felt hollow. Loyalty had its limits, especially when rent was due.

The decline continued through August and into September. Friday shows that once drew three hundred were now struggling to break one-fifty. We were barely covering the cost of renting the Armory.

Stan grew increasingly desperate, trying everything from two-for-one ticket offers to bringing in questionable "special attractions" that further strained our budget.

THUNDERdome had popped the house a touch, but it was still disappointing given the spectacle of the match. Eight wrestlers inside a steel cage, no holds barred, only one man walks out victorious.

Mike's win didn't exactly set the world on fire.

"What about another hardcore match?" Stan suggested during one particularly bleak booking conversation. "The fans went nuts for Sy Reaper."

"No they didn't. In fact, half of them walked out." If he could exaggerate, so could I. "We totally lost that family with the kids who'd been coming every week for a year."

Stan tapped his pen against the table. "What about a big

name?"

"You've got to pay big names," I said dismissively.

"I bet I could get an old-timer to come in on the cheap."

"Who?" I asked, not bothering to hide my skepticism.

Stan ignored the question. "We'll figure something out," he said finally. "We always do."

We both knew that wasn't true anymore.

The first sign of real dissension in the ranks came when Stan started delaying payouts. First by a day, then a week. The boys grumbled openly, but almost all of them accepted it. We did lose Bad Brad to UWA, though.

"Can't blame him," Mike said after Brad's departure. "Man's got kids."

My own financial situation had grown more precarious since my standoff with Eric. The performance improvement plan had effectively killed any chances of advancement at Silvertech, and I assumed my job was in jeopardy. I'd started updating my resume. The thought of job hunting at my age filled me with dread.

As Halloween and Thanksgiving came, even Stan's optimism began to fade. He spent more time in his office, making desperate calls to promoters in neighboring states, trying to organize talent exchanges or even inter-promotional storylines—anything to inject some life into our dying promotion.

I was in the warehouse office early one Wednesday, sorting through the dwindling stack of merchandise we had left to sell, when I noticed an official-looking envelope on top of my table. It was addressed to Stan, with "CERTIFIED MAIL" stamped across the front and "OPEN IMMEDIATELY" in bold red letters.

My stomach tightened as I picked it up. It had already been

opened, the contents hastily stuffed back inside. I hesitated only briefly before pulling out the letter.

It was from our landlord at the warehouse—a formal notice of eviction. According to the document, Stan had missed three months of rent payments. We had until the end of January to vacate the premises.

Three months. Stan had been hiding this for three entire months.

The door opened behind me, and Stan froze when he saw the envelope on the desk.

"So, you saw?" His voice was oddly flat.

"It was sitting right there," I said. "Three months, Stan? You haven't paid rent in three months, and you didn't think to mention it?"

He set his coffee down. "I was handling it."

"Handling it how? We can barely make payroll. Where exactly was three months of back rent going to come from?"

Stan waved his hand vaguely. "I've got some things in the works. Potential investors."

"What investors?" I asked, skepticism evident in my voice. "DiMarco was the only person crazy enough to want in on this business, and you drove him away."

"DiMarco," Stan spat, some of his old fire returning. "That's your solution? The guy who stole my champion and half my roster?"

"At least he pays his wrestlers and his rent," I shot back.

Stan's face darkened. "Whose side are you on, Luke?"

It was the same question he'd asked when Joey quit, when I'd told him to go fuck himself. But this time, the answer felt different.

"Come on, Stan," I said, more tired than angry. "When do we face reality? The promotion is finished."

"We are not done." Stan stood up, his voice rising. "I've come back from worse than this."

"When? When have you ever come back from worse than this? We've lost half our roster. Attendance is in the toilet. We're being evicted. What exactly is your plan here?"

Stan opened his mouth to respond, then closed it again. For a moment, he looked lost—the veneer of the confident promoter cracking to reveal the frightened old man beneath.

"I've given my life to the business," he said quietly. "Forty-plus years. What am I supposed to do?"

His vulnerability caught me off guard.

"I don't know," I said honestly. "But pretending everything's fine isn't helping."

Stan slumped back into his chair, staring at the ceiling.

"We could move to a smaller venue," he said finally. "Cut down to one show a month until things turn around."

"Maybe," I said, though neither of us believed it. "But first we need to tell the boys. They deserve to know what's happening."

"Give me til Friday to figure out what we're doing."

I left him there, sitting in his office surrounded by the artifacts of a lifetime in wrestling—faded posters, replica championship belts from defunct promotions, photographs of a younger Stan grappling with opponents long since retired or dead.

Walking to my car, I caught sight of a UWA flyer taped to a nearby telephone pole. The glossy paper featured Trent holding their championship belt, a smirking Tony DiMarco standing beside him. My phone buzzed with a text from Joey:

Still on for the Wing Place tonight?

Yeah. I need a beer. Or twenty.

That bad?

Worse.

Forty-Six

It was Sunday morning and I was running behind for the meeting Stan had called for the entire roster.

Chuck, our sound guy, was pulling into the parking lot of the warehouse at the same time. He'd been with the promotion almost as long as I had, handling the music cues and audio for our shows. He threw his car in park and hopped out, practically running toward my car with his phone in hand.

"Luke! You need to see this."

"What is it?"

"Just watch."

He played a video. A local news channel's logo was in the bottom corner. A female reporter was standing outside the Millersport Sports Arena, UWA's main venue. Behind her, red and blue lights flashed from several police cars.

"...shocking arrest at tonight's professional wrestling event," the reporter was saying. "UWA champion Trent Howard was taken into custody immediately following the main event match."

I felt a chill run down my spine as I watched the footage of

Trent being led out of the building in handcuffs, still in his wrestling gear. Officers guided him toward a waiting cruiser.

"Howard, 24, faces multiple charges including vehicular assault and leaving the scene of an accident. According to police, Howard struck another vehicle late Friday night, injuring two people—including a passenger in his own vehicle—before fleeing the scene. He was identified through surveillance footage and taken into custody at tonight's professional wrestling event."

"Can you believe it?" Chuck's eyes were wide with the excitement of breaking news. "There's more footage on Twitter. Cops waited till he was walking back from the ring, then cuffed him in front of everyone. DiMarco looked like he was gonna pass out."

Stan had called everyone to the warehouse. Speculation of what he was going to say was rampant. Were we shutting down? Was he selling the company? Even ridiculous questions like were we merging with the UWA had surfaced.

Nobody expected good news. They didn't know about the eviction notice and they didn't know that without a training facility—and the income from the wrestling school—the promotion was all but finished.

I walked in and the boys were buzzing. "Luke! Did you hear?" Mike asked.

"Just now."

"Does Stan know?"

"I don't know."

Stan was in his office, glancing at his watch. He'd spent the morning working on his speech, going over what he would say to the boys. I saw his notes scribbled on the back of an envelope—phrases like "temporary setback" and "restructuring period." They would see right through that, no matter how good of a promo Stan cut today.

He cleared his throat behind me. "About time you got here."

"Stan," I said, closing the door behind me. "Do you know?"

"Know what?"

I loaded the video Chuck had shown me, held up my phone, and showed him the paused image of Trent in handcuffs.

Stan's eyes widened as he took the phone, thumb pressing play.

"When did this happen?" he whispered.

"Last night."

Stan handed the phone back to me. He put the envelope with his scrawls on it in his back pocket.

"Well, let's get this meeting started."

"Boys. And lady, of course," he said as he smiled at Amber. "I want to talk about where we're headed as a promotion. Some of you might have heard rumors about SWP," he continued. "Some of it is true. Some of it isn't."

The wrestlers exchanged glances.

"I won't sugarcoat it. We've been struggling. But wrestling is cyclical." Stan's eyes gleamed with a fire I hadn't seen in weeks. "And it appears that today, the cycle starts over."

He gestured for my phone. Stan held it up, showing the screen to the gathered wrestlers.

"This, gentlemen, is what happens when you build your promotion on bullshit. UWA's golden boy got drunk, hit another vehicle, hurt two people—including the girl he was with—and then ran. That's Tony DiMarco's champion."

The wrestlers were chattering. Some had already heard; others were just finding out, shaking their heads.

Stan continued. "And now DiMarco's paying the price for backing the wrong horse." He handed the phone back to me, then stood up straight. "So, here's what we're going to do."

I caught his eye. The eviction notice was still real. Our financial problems hadn't magically disappeared because Trent got arrested. But Stan was in full babyface mode now.

"We're going to capitalize on this," Stan declared. "Next month, we're running a special event. Something big. Something that will bring back the fans who've drifted to UWA."

"What kind of special event?" Stew asked.

Stan paused dramatically, looking around the room. "My retirement show."

I was shocked. From the stunned expressions on the wrestlers' faces, they were equally surprised.

"That's right, boys," Stan continued. "After all of these years in this business, I'm hanging up my boots. One last big event, a celebration of everything we've built, and then I'm passing the torch to Luke." He pointed at me as he said it.

This declaration practically gave me a heart attack. We'd never discussed anything remotely close to this. Was he expecting me to buy him out? Was he giving me the promotion? And what would I do with a failing business that would have no headquarters in a few days?

"We'll bring back some legends," Stan was saying, already building the card in his head. "Guys I've trained over the years. The fans will eat this up."

Chuck appeared beside me. "Pretty crazy timing, huh? Just when things looked their worst."

"Yeah," I said distantly. "Crazy timing."

After the meeting broke up, I noticed Amber scrolling on her phone.

"You're quiet," I said, approaching her.

She looked up, a humorless smile crossing her face. "What is there to say?"

I pulled up a folding chair and sat across from her. "Tell me what you're thinking."

"I mean, we all saw this coming. Not this specifically," she clarified. "But I knew something wasn't right with Trent."

"I mean, sure. But yeah, I didn't expect it to be this bad."

"Well, I told Stan—"

"Wait, what?"

"I told Stan that the guy was bad news. I had girls tell me that they wouldn't wrestle here if Trent was on the show. That, and the way he was interacting with some of the female fans was really inappropriate."

"Wow. Why didn't you come to me?"

"Because I knew he was Stan's boy, not yours."

"Amber—" My stomach tightened. "What did Stan say?"

"What do you think he said?" Amber's voice was flat. "'Trent's just being friendly.' 'Good for business to have engagement with the audience.' 'Don't make mountains out of molehills.' Same shit women hear every time we raise a concern about this stuff."

"I'm sorry," I said, not sure what else to offer. "I should have—"

"No. Stan should have." Amber cut me off, though her tone was gentle. "But it's bigger than Stan. It's the system that protects talent at the expense of everything else. Stan did it. DiMarco did it. The whole business does it."

I didn't know what to say.

She shrugged. "Maybe next time someone raises a concern, people will listen before it becomes a headline."

As she headed toward the exit, she paused. "You know what the saddest part is? That girl in the car with him—she probably loved wrestling. And now?" She shook her head. "Now it's ruined. And you guys wonder why we choose the bear."

Forty-Seven

Throughout the day, I monitored the news on my phone. I pulled up another video from a different station.

"...This is a developing story about the arrest of a local wrestling champion..."

I clicked the volume buttons to make the audio louder.

"Trent Howard faces multiple charges including OWI causing serious bodily injury and two counts of leaving the scene of an accident, a Level 3 felony under Indiana law. According to police, Howard hit another vehicle, injuring both the driver and his own passenger, before speeding away."

They showed fan footage of Trent being led out of the Miller-sport Sports Arena in handcuffs. "Howard, who performed under his real name, was suspended by UWA promoter and local car dealer Tony DiMarco, who issued a statement saying the organization had cut ties..."

"Karma's a real bitch." Stan's voice came from behind me. He stood in the doorway to his office, arms crossed, a look of grim satisfaction on his face.

"Jesus, Stan! Is that your takeaway here?"

"What? I'm stating facts." He peered over my should, eyes fixed on the screen where Tony DiMarco was now giving a hastily arranged press conference outside his dealership.

"...want to make it absolutely clear that UWA has no tolerance for this kind of behavior," DiMarco was saying, his usual confidence gone. "We are cooperating fully with authorities and have suspended Mr. Howard indefinitely..."

Stan snorted. "Look at him squirm. Six months ago, he was poaching our talent, now he's scrambling to save his own ass." His eyes gleamed with the unmistakable look of a promoter spotting an opportunity in chaos.

"This isn't about us versus them," I said, switching off the TV. "Think about the guy who got hit. And the girl in the car with him."

"Well, of course. But still—that fucking DiMarco deserves everything he's getting."

My phone buzzed with a text from Joey:

You seeing this Trent stuff?

I typed back:

Yeah. Crazy.

"Stan, this is gonna hurt all of us."

"I hope not," he said.

"People hear 'wrestler arrested,' they don't distinguish between promotions. We're all guilty by association."

The story gained traction as the week went on. On Wednesday, the local paper ran a story with the headline "LOCAL WRESTLING

CHAMPION ARRESTED IN HIT AND RUN." The article mentioned our promotion alongside UWA, noting that Trent had "previously performed for Stanley Weizenschmidt's wrestling organization" before joining DiMarco's company.

Stan slammed the newspaper on the desk. "They're making it sound like we did something wrong! I'm calling their editor."

"Don't," I advised. "You'll make it a bigger story. Let it go."

But Stan was already dialing, prepared to unleash his righteous indignation on some guy's voicemail.

I stepped outside, needing air and distance from Stan's theatrics. Mike was leaned against his car, a thin curl of smoke rising from a cigarette between his tattooed fingers.

"You're early today," I said to him.

"Hell of a thing," he said, offering me the pack. I declined with a wave. His weathered face looked older in the harsh parking lot light, the scars from years in the business more pronounced.

"I just hope he doesn't take us down with him," I said.

Mike exhaled a long stream of smoke, watching it dissipate in the cool air. "We'll be alright. Stan always lands on his feet."

FORTY-EIGHT

Friday's show at the Elmwood Armory drew four hundred and two fans—our best in months.

Stan had called the editor of the newspaper but instead of screaming at him, he turned on the charm. He gave an interview emphasizing that we'd "parted ways" with Trent months before his arrest, carefully avoiding any mention of the fact that we'd pushed him as our champion right up until the moment he defected to UWA. He spoke about our commitment to "family-friendly entertainment" and our "zero-tolerance policy for inappropriate behavior," as if these had always been core tenets of our operation rather than hastily adopted positions in the wake of scandal.

Cynical and self-serving, but it worked.

UWA cancelled their upcoming shows. DiMarco's statement made it clear they were severing ties with Trent completely, despite the careful language about "suspension pending investigation." Tony gave several interviews expressing shock and dismay, claiming he had no knowledge of Trent's alleged behavior and would never have hired him had he known. And suddenly, his dealership started sponsoring little league teams and making donations to child welfare organizations.

Before the show, Stan gathered everyone around him in the locker room. "Alright, listen up. I know everybody's talking about what happened with Trent."

The guys were quiet.

"But I want to make one thing crystal clear," Stan continued, his voice growing more forceful. "What he did was awful. But this is not who *we* are. This is not what *our promotion* stands for. And I will not let that piece of garbage drag us down with him. Moving forward, any wrestler representing this promotion will be held to a standard of conduct on and off the road. You drink, you don't drive. You call an Uber or you find another way home. This is not negotiable."

These were rules that he and I had worked on together, but we both knew they carried more weight coming directly from him.

Jim spoke up. "Think this shit will affect our attendance?"

Stan's eyes brightened. "Actually, things are looking OK tonight. So, maybe it will help us. But we need to position ourselves as the clean, family-friendly option. When people think of us, I want them to think about Apple Pie."

"Pie?" Stew asked.

"American as Apple Pie. People love that shit."

After the meeting, Stan pulled me aside. "I'm going out there and cutting a promo to address this head-on."

"Is that wise?" I asked. "Drawing more attention to it?"

"We can't ignore it," Stan insisted. "Every fan in the building will be thinking about it. Better to acknowledge it, condemn it, and move on."

He had a point. Silence could be interpreted as indifference or, worse, complicity.

"Fine," I conceded. "But keep it brief and dignified. This isn't an angle."

Stan looked almost offended. "I know what I'm doing, Luke."

Before the show, Stan asked me, "Hey, you think Joey would do one more match at the retirement show?"

"I'll ask him." The conversation was brief but productive: he agreed to appear but only if his opponent was experienced and safe. His only other condition was that we donate a portion of the gate to a MADD.

"Rachel made a good point about this. It's important that we not just condemn this kind of behavior but actively work against it," he explained.

"I agree."

"Luke," Joey's voice grew serious. "This is definitely my last match."

"Understood," I assured him. "One night, one match, that's it."

After the first match, Stan took the microphone. The crowd fell silent as he stepped to the center of the ring. True to his word, he kept it dignified—condemning Trent's alleged actions without mentioning him by name, reaffirming our commitment to creating a safe environment for fans of all ages, announcing the new policies we'd enacted. It was tasteful, appropriate, and completely unlike Stan's usual bombastic style.

"And now," he concluded, "let's talk about next Friday night." The crowd popped and Stan waited for them to settle. "We've got a hell of a lineup! First of all, you'll see—in action—that no good turncoat, Jim 'The Hammer' Tanner!"

The crowd booed. Jim had recently turned heel, mostly because we were looking for anything that might drive attendance.

"He'll be going one on one with... former SWP heavyweight champion, the returning Joey Davis!"

The crowd was louder than I expected.

Stan continued his promo. "And, making a special appearance... one of my former tag team partners... the legendary JACKIE SAVAGE!"

This was pretty big. Our old school fans were excited about seeing the old-timer.

"Tickets are on sale now. We'll have more announcements as the night goes on, but I'd also like to announce that a portion of all ticket proceeds will be donated to Mothers Against Drunk Driving. Because in wrestling, like in life, we have a responsibility to protect the community and hold ourselves to a higher standard."

I almost believed he meant it.

FORTY-NINE

"WE HAVE A PROBLEM," Stan said on Monday evening. "I just got off the phone with Jackie Savage's people. He's not coming."

This was a blow. Jackie had been advertised as the main "legend" at the retirement show, his name prominently featured on all promotional materials. He was the closest thing to a star we had on the card.

"Why not? I thought you had a deal."

"He got a better offer," Stan said bitterly. "Some convention in Cleveland is paying him triple what we can afford."

"Can't he do both? Cleveland's not that far."

Stan shook his head. "Wouldn't be worth it for him financially to miss Friday there to do our show."

"So, what do we do? It's too late to reprint posters or programs."

"Well, we need another legend," he said slowly. "Someone the fans will recognize, someone with drawing power."

"Like who? Most of the guys from your era are long gone. No offense."

Stan ignored it. "You know who we should bring in . . ."

"You don't mean—"

Stan said one word. "Yep."

"Victor Koslov? The Russian Nightmare?" I raised an eyebrow. "Are you OK with that? Will he do it?"

"For the right price."

"Which we can't afford," I pointed out. "If we couldn't meet Jackie's new price, how can we possibly afford Victor?"

"I've got some money set aside in an emergency fund."

I shook my head. If Stan had an "emergency fund," why hadn't he used it to pay the warehouse rent and avoid eviction? But I knew better than to ask.

"Even if we can afford him, what makes you think he'd agree? You're not exactly his favorite person, right?"

"Money talks," Stan said confidently. "And he's got to be as curious about this 'retirement' as everyone else. The chance to see old Stan Weizenschmidt bow out of the business? Hell, he might do it for free."

Even after fifteen years, the thought of seeing two of my favorites together one more time gave me a charge.

"I don't think he'll come," I said, managing my expectations.

"Luke, he's my best friend in the business. He'll come if I ask him."

"Wait. He's your best friend?"

Stan just smiled.

"So, you're telling me the thirty-year blood feud was... what? Mostly for show?"

Stan chuckled. "Kid, in this business, a good story is worth more than the truth."

"Wow."

"So, now," Stan said, his eyes glinting with that familiar promotional spark, "now we finish the story. One last time."

FIFTY

"I APPRECIATE your time this afternoon, especially on a Friday,"
I said as I closed the door to Eric's office and sat down across from
him. The glass walls now felt like a fishbowl. Everyone in the open
workspace beyond could see us, but not hear us. "Thanks for
fitting me in."

Eric settled into his chair, face unreadable. "So. You wanted to
talk?"

I slid the envelope across his desk. "This is my resignation
letter."

If Eric was surprised, he didn't show it. He picked up the envelope but didn't open it, studying me instead. "I can't say I didn't
see this coming. But are you sure?"

"I've been offered another position."

"Oh?" A flicker of curiosity crossed his face. "Where?"

"Heartland Products. I'll be their new IT Director."

Now Eric did look surprised. "That's... unexpected. They're
not exactly known for their technological innovation."

"They're looking to change that," I replied. "That's why they're
bringing me in."

Eric nodded slowly, turning the envelope over in his hands. "Director title. That's a step up. Congratulations."

"Thank you."

Several weeks ago, after I'd discovered the eviction notice, I met Joey at The Wing Place. We had a conversation that set this all in motion.

Joey was waiting at our usual spot, two beers already on the table. I slid into the chair across from him.

"You look like hell," Joey observed, taking a drink.

"Feel like it too," I admitted, taking a grateful sip. "Things aren't great. But I don't want to talk about wrestling. How's the new job treating you?"

Joey's face lit up. "It's good, man. Really good. Normal hours, weekends off, benefits... I feel like I've discovered some secret that normal people have been keeping from us."

I laughed. "Sounds nice."

"It is." Joey hesitated, then leaned forward. "That's why I wanted to meet tonight. There's an opening at Heartland I thought you might be interested in."

"Me?"

"The current guy's retiring next month. They're looking for someone with management experience who can modernize their systems."

"I don't know, Joey. I'm not exactly a manager—"

"Luke," Joey cut me off, "you've been running Stan's entire operation for fifteen years. You're exactly what they're looking for. You'd be the Director of IT."

I took another sip of beer. "I don't know if I'm qualified."

Joey grinned. "Look, I've been talking you up to Rachel's cousin, who happens to be their HR manager. They're more interested in someone who can solve problems than someone with a perfect resume."

"Huh..."

"Just think about it," Joey said.

Back in Eric's office, an awkward silence had fallen between us. Ten years as colleagues, and neither of us seemed to know what to say.

"Look, Luke," Eric finally spoke, setting the envelope down. "I know things have been strained since the performance improvement plan. But if this is about negotiating a better position here—"

I shook my head. "It's not. I appreciate everything Silvertech has done for me. But it's time for a change."

Eric leaned back in his chair, regarding me thoughtfully. "You know, when I first put you on that PIP, I thought it would force you to choose—us or that wrestling thing. Guess that backfired. I'm gonna miss you."

"Thanks, Eric. For everything. Really."

FIFTY-ONE

The Armory hummed with anticipation. Every seat was filled, with standing room only along the back wall. Five hundred and twelve paying customers—our largest crowd ever. They came for different reasons: loyal fans supporting the promotion one last time, curiosity seekers drawn by the spectacle of Stan's retirement, lapsed viewers returning for a dose of nostalgia. Some, undoubtedly, were there because of the scandal that had engulfed UWA, seeking an alternative to the tainted product across town.

Whatever their motivation, it created an electric atmosphere.

Backstage was organized chaos. Stan was everywhere at once, making last-minute adjustments, greeting returning alumni, and projecting confidence despite the visible tension in his shoulders.

He cleared his throat, drawing the attention of the locker room. The wrestlers were dressed in their gear, some stretching, others taping wrists or adjusting boots—the usual pre-show ritual playing out for what might be the final time.

"Before we go out there," Stan began, his voice lacking its usual bombast, "I want to say something to all of you."

The room quieted. The wrestlers leaned forward, their movements sending a chorus of creaks through the flimsy metal folding chairs.

"This business..." Stan paused. "This business takes more than it gives. Always has. But you boys have stuck with me through the worst of it."

Stan turned to Jim, who was methodically wrapping his knees in the corner. "Jim. You've been with me almost from the beginning. You had offers from bigger promotions. Better money. But you stayed, and you made this place legitimate when we couldn't afford much else. You gave us credibility. You made kids who didn't deserve to be in the same ring with you look like stars. Thank you."

Jim nodded. "Happy to do it, Stan."

Stan shifted his gaze to Mike. "Bruiser, you scary mother fucker. You brought international experience to our little territory. Japan. Mexico. You could've gone back anytime, but you stayed, taught these kids what real wrestling looks like. Not the flashy garbage they see on TV, but the real deal."

Mike, normally quick with a comeback, simply touched his finger to his lips and tapped his heart.

Stan looked at me, and I braced myself.

"Luke. For fifteen years, you've kept this operation from falling apart. Solved problems I didn't even know existed. Making miracles happen on shoestring budgets. And putting up with my bullshit." Stan shook his head slightly. "I'm not easy to work with. I know that. But you never walked away, even when you probably should have."

I gave a small nod of acknowledgment and felt my face blush a little. Joey patted me on the back.

"I could not have done this without you. Know that."

I looked down at my shoes, so that I wouldn't cry.

Stan's gaze swept the room, taking in the rest of the roster.

"The rest of you—whether you've been here ten years or ten months—each of you has had a part in what we've built here."

He paused, his eyes finding the mountain of a man sitting quietly in the back corner. "Oh. There he is. How could I miss you, you big bastard."

Stew looked up, surprised at being singled out last. All eyes turned to him and his mammoth frame hunched uncomfortably.

"Twenty years," Stan said, his voice taking on a gentleness I'd rarely heard. "Twenty years you've been putting your body on the line for this promotion. You've never complained, even when your knee gave out. You never asked for more money. Never threatened to walk when things got tough."

Stan's voice softened further. "I've had flashier talents. Guys who thought they were superstars. Even guys who did become superstars." He paused. "But I never had anyone more loyal or more professional than you, Stewart."

Stew didn't react, but he did smile.

"Remember that blizzard in '09?" Stan continued. "Power was out at the venue, the roads barely passable. Half the roster cancelled. But there was Stew, two hours early to help shovel the parking lot. And then he worked two matches because we were short-handed."

Stew stared at the floor, his massive hands fidgeting in his lap.

Stan's voice cracked just a little. "You never asked for the spot-light," Stan said. "But you've always deserved it the most. I will be forever grateful to you. And I'm proud to call you my friend."

There was a single tear running down Stan's cheek. I'd never seen that. Ever.

He wiped it away. "Don't get used to this," Stan added, his gruffness returning slightly as the room laughed. "I'm not going soft. But if this really is the end... I just wanted to say thank you. For everything."

Several of us were holding back tears now. Mike broke the

tension, clapping Stew on his massive shoulder. "About damn time someone put you over, big man."

More laughter rippled through the room, and Stew's face broke into that gentle smile—the one that had remained unchanged through injured knees, rope burns, and decades of taking bumps for barely any money.

"Thanks, boss," he said simply, then added, "Just did what needed doing."

FIFTY-TWO

JOEY SAT IN THE CORNER, hands wrapped, boots laced, ready for his first match in months. He looked different—calmer, more centered than I remembered.

"You ready?" I asked, approaching with clipboard in hand.

"I am. Did Victor really show up?"

"He did. He and Stan have been locked in Stan's office since he got here. Ten-year-old me is excited to see him and Stan in the same ring together again."

Stan had given me the rundown. Victor would come to the ring during Stan's retirement speech, say a few words about their history together, and they'd symbolically bury the hatchet after thirty years of animosity. It was the kind of moment wrestling fans lived for—real-life rivals setting aside their differences, if only for one night.

I didn't trust it for a second.

"Is Rachel here?" I asked, changing the subject.

"Yeah, with her Dad. She wouldn't miss it. My Mom came, too."

"Good. That's good. Listen, Joey. I want you to know how much—"

I was interrupted by the sound of the national anthem, something Stan insisted be played before every show. The song was followed by the announcer's voice booming through the PA system. "Ladies and gentlemen, welcome to Stanley Weizenschmidt Presents: The Final Bell!"

Joey smiled. "You don't need to thank me."

I clapped him on the shoulder. "Well, I'll buy you a beer later."

I found my usual spot by the curtain. The opening match was underway and everything was going according to plan. The crowd —all five hundred plus—were loud, which always made it easier for the boys to perform.

I spotted Rachel in the third row, sitting next to her dad and a woman I assumed was Joey's mother. Something caught the light on Rachel's left hand—a small diamond ring.

That little shit, I thought. *He proposed and didn't tell me.*

We put the title match in the middle of the show. Stew and Mike had good chemistry and at the end of it, Stew stood victorious in the center of the ring having won his first ever SWP Heavyweight Title.

Scripted or not, it was the reward he deserved for his loyalty.

Once the celebration was over, the show continued. The ring announcer climbed into the ring and said, "And now, ladies and gentlemen, from Minneapolis, Minnesota, this is JIM "THE HAMMER" TANNER!" His music hit, he walked to the ring with a cockiness that told me he was having a blast playing the heel.

Once his music faded, the crowd began a rhythmic chant: "JO-EY! JO-EY! JO-EY!" They remembered. The super brief tenure as champion, months away from the ring—none of it mattered. They wanted to see him one more time.

"Go get 'em, kid," I said as he paced and dumped a water bottle on his head to wet his hair.

His music hit and the crowd erupted. He stepped through the curtain, his face breaking into a smile as the wall of sound hit him. The people were welcoming back someone they'd genuinely missed.

The match itself was everything I'd hoped it would be. Joey showed no ring rust, his movements as fluid and crisp, just like he'd never left. Jim, the consummate professional, guided the narrative masterfully, building from tentative exchanges to high-impact sequences that had the crowd gasping and cheering in all the right places.

They told a simple story: the veteran testing the younger man, finding him worthy, then pushing him to his limits in a contest of skill and heart. And when that didn't work, Jim used cheap shots, heel tactics, and still he couldn't keep the babyface down.

I'd fought with Stan about the finish. Knowing Joey wouldn't be returning, I insisted that Jim go over. Stan agreed. "Normally, that's the right call." And then he said, "But not tonight."

I let it go.

When Joey finally hit his signature move—a diving cross body from the top rope, executed masterfully—the crowd rose, counting along with the referee:

One! Two! Three!

The bell rang, and the Armory erupted. Joey stood in the center of the ring, arms raised, beaming. Jim, selling exhaustion, rolled to the outside, and Joey celebrated his victory.

When they both returned backstage, sweaty and breathing hard but grinning from ear to ear, they were greeted by a round of applause from the assembled wrestlers.

"Hell of a match, kid," Mike said, embracing Joey in a one-armed hug. "Way to go out on top."

Joey accepted the praise with his usual humility, thanking Jim for the match. In the midst of this, Stan appeared, looking uncharacteristically nervous. "Raffle time," he announced. "Retirement speech is next. Luke, I need you to introduce me."

"Me?" I hadn't been expecting this.

"Yes," Stan said, his voice softening slightly, "you're the one who's kept this place running. And they're gonna need to know that you're keeping things going once I'm gone." We still hadn't discussed what was going to happen with the business—whether he was just giving it to me or expecting me to buy it from him.

I was afraid to ask and he didn't offer any details.

"And Joey," Stan continued, "I'd like you at ringside too."

"Oh, OK. Sure, Stan. Whatever you need."

Stan went back to his office and Joey asked, "Why does he want me down there?"

"I have no idea, but you know Stan..."

"I saw Victor warming up earlier, stretching like he's planning to get physical."

Victor Koslov, like Stan, was in his sixties, well past the age where "getting physical" was advisable, especially without proper preparation.

"Old habits die hard, I guess," I said. "But they're just doing mic work."

Chuck stuck his head through the curtain. "It's time," he said.

I took a deep breath, straightened my shoulders, and made my way to the entrance position, mentally reviewing what I would say to introduce Stan. After fifteen years by his side, surely I could find the right words to send him off.

FIFTY-THREE

THE ANNOUNCER SAID, "Ladies and Gentlemen, please welcome the SWP Operations Manager, Luke Anderson." My theme song played—a simple, nondescript song we used for stuff like this—and I stepped through the curtain to polite applause. The crowd knew me primarily as a background figure, the clipboard-wielding authority who occasionally appeared to break up a brawl or came out when things got too real.

None of them knew what I really did.

And that was fine. Wrestling wasn't about the behind-the-scenes players; it was about the characters, the stories, the spectacle.

I took the microphone from the ring announcer and stepped to the center of the ring. The crowd quieted, expectant.

"Ladies and gentlemen," I began, "for over fifteen years, I've had the privilege—and sometimes the challenge—of working alongside one of professional wrestling's most legendary figures. He's been a wrestler, a promoter, a mentor, a visionary, and occasionally, a royal pain in the ass."

This drew laughs from the audience, particularly from the

wrestlers who'd come out from behind the curtain to watch. I continued, balancing respect with honesty, tracing Stan's career from his days as a territorial wrestler through his transition to promoting, highlighting his contributions to the business we both loved.

The speech was easy. Despite all his flaws, Stan had dedicated his life to professional wrestling. I understood the sacrifices required to do that better than anyone.

"And so," I concluded, "whatever comes next, tonight marks the end of an era. Ladies and gentlemen, please welcome for one last time—Stanley Weizenschmidt . . . STAN THE MAN!"

Stan's music blared through the PA system and he emerged through the curtain to a rousing ovation. He'd dressed up tonight: pressed suit, hair combed neatly back, and the swagger he was known for.

As he entered the ring, Stan embraced me briefly—a gesture that caught me off guard. Then he took the microphone, his face solemn as the music faded and the crowd grew quiet once more. I hopped out of the ring and down to the floor next to where Joey was standing.

"Thank you, Luke," he began. "For those kind words, and for everything else over the years." He turned to face the fans directly. "And thank you all for coming tonight. Looking out at this packed house, seeing so many familiar faces... it means more than I can express."

Stan spoke for several minutes, recounting his journey through the business, thanking various wrestlers and personalities who'd influenced him, acknowledging the challenges the promotion had faced in recent years. He even resisted heaving one last insult to Tony DiMarco.

"But every journey must end," he said finally. "And mine has reached its conclusion. So tonight, I officially announce my retirement from professional wrestling."

The crowd responded with mostly applause and more than a few boos. Stan nodded, accepting both.

"Before I go, though, there's one piece of unfinished business." He paused dramatically. "As many of you know, there's been... I've had bad blood with a guy for thirty years. Thirty years of animosity, thirty years of bitterness. That ends tonight as well."

On cue, Victor Koslov's music began to play—an old Soviet-themed anthem that dated back to his days as a Cold War heel. Victor emerged through the curtain, his imposing frame still impressive even at his age. He wore street clothes—jeans and a tight black t-shirt that strained against his barrel chest—and moved with the deliberate gait of a man conscious of old injuries. His face, weather-beaten and lined, bore no expression as he made his way to the ring.

The audience erupted at seeing him. Once a star, always a star.

Victor entered the ring, never taking his eyes off Stan. For a long moment, they simply stared at each other, decades of resentment and rivalry hanging in the air between them. The crowd was buzzing, the legendary rivalry still drawing heat.

Finally, Victor took a second microphone from the ring announcer.

"Stanley," Victor began, his voice still carrying the faint accent that had once been exaggerated for his Russian character. "It has been many years."

"Too many," Stan agreed.

Victor surveyed the crowd thoughtfully. "Do these people know our history? The stolen money? The betrayal?"

Stan's smile tightened. "Ancient history, Victor. Water under the bridge. That's why you're here, right? To put the past behind us."

Victor considered this. "Yes. The past should stay in the past. But truth . . . truth must be acknowledged before it can be forgiven."

"Victor," Stan said, a warning in his tone. "Let's not—"

"You robbed me," Victor continued, ignoring Stan's interruption. "Took my share of our earnings, slept with my wife, then told everyone it was I who had betrayed you."

The crowd murmured, not having expected this level of real-life drama. Stan's face reddened, his composure slipping.

This wasn't what I was expecting either.

"That's not how it happened," he snapped, reaching for Victor's microphone. Victor held it away from him.

"For thirty years, I have carried the reputation of a traitor, a thief while you built your little empire here." Victor's eyes hardened. "Tonight, you wish me to shake your hand? To absolve you in front of these people? So, you can retire with clear conscience?"

Stan was fully flustered now. Off mic, he said, "This isn't the time or place, Victor. We agreed—"

"I agreed to nothing," Victor cut in. "I came to hear you admit the truth. One time, before you leave the business. That is my price for peace."

The Armory fell silent, the crowd holding its breath. This didn't feel like a scripted angle; the tension was too real, the emotions too raw.

Victor took a step toward Stan and Stan did not step backwards. They started jawing at one another, while the crowd began to come alive.

Joey climbed onto the apron and into the ring.

He stood between Stan and Victor. He radiated a calm sense of authority that seemed out of place given his youth and relative inexperience. He took Stan's mic. "I know I'm not part of this history," he said, his voice steady. "But if tonight is about endings and new beginnings, maybe it's time for both of you to let go of the past. Whatever happened thirty years ago... does it really matter now? Look around."

Joey looked around at the packed venue, to the fans hanging

on every word. "These people came to celebrate what professional wrestling has meant to them. What both of you have contributed to it. Not to witness old grudges being rehashed."

Stan and Victor looked almost embarrassed, like schoolboys caught fighting in the yard. The raw emotion that had been building just moments before began to dissipate, replaced by a grudging acknowledgment of Joey's point.

"The kid is right," Victor conceded finally. "This is not the place." He turned to Stan. "Perhaps we speak privately, later. Resolve what can be resolved."

Stan was visibly relieved by this de-escalation. "I'd like that, Victor. Really."

To everyone's surprise, Victor extended his hand. After a moment's hesitation, Stan took it. The crowd erupted in applause —not for the somewhat awkward handshake itself, but for what it represented: the possibility of reconciliation, of healing old wounds, of moving forward.

As the applause continued, Stan raised his microphone once more. "Thank you, Victor. And thank you, Joey. You're right. Tonight should be about celebration, not—"

Before Stan could finish his sentence, Mike "The Bruiser" Alvarez's music hit. He exploded through the curtain and charged toward the ring. He climbed through the ropes and stood between the two veterans. The crowd was confused. Then, all of a sudden, Mike blindsided Joey with a clothesline that sent him crashing to the canvas.

The crowd shrieked and booed as Mike began stomping on Joey's chest. Stan and Victor scrambled away from the violence.

I stood frozen at ringside, my brain struggling to process what was happening. This wasn't in any rundown I'd heard.

Stan finally stepped toward Mike, shouting at him to stop. Mike turned, and with a snarl, shoved Stan backward into Victor.

This upset the Russian and the two older men began shoving each other, blaming each other for the chaos.

The Armory erupted. Mike had Joey locked in a painful-looking submission hold. Joey's face registered distress as he struggled to break free. The referees had all run down to the ring, trying to break up the fighting. They were not successful.

Then the arena lights went out.

An entrance theme we hadn't heard in months began to play. The crowd's reaction was instantaneous and deafening.

The lights came back on and Kole the Krusher—the champion whose career-threatening injury had changed everything—stood center ring, fully recovered and ready for vengeance.

The crowd lost its collective mind. Mike released Joey and scrambled to his feet, but too late—Kole was on him in a flash, delivering a flurry of strikes that drove Mike to the corner.

My jaw dropped. I had no idea Kole was medically cleared, let alone that he'd be here tonight.

As Kole and Mike brawled across the ring, Stan and Victor continued their own heated exchange, escalating from shoves to wild, exaggerated punches.

Through it all, Joey had rolled to the edge of the ring, selling his injuries from Mike's attack. As Kole finally delivered his finisher to Mike—a devastating-looking piledriver—Joey pulled himself up on the ropes, recovering just enough to witness the heroic rescue.

When the dust settled, Mike had been driven from the ring, Stan and Victor stood on opposite sides glaring at each other, and Kole stood triumphant in the center, helping Joey to his feet. The two shook hands to thunderous applause.

"Well, ladies and gentlemen," Stan said, taking back the microphone, "I don't think this is over. No, in fact, I think we need to settle some scores. So—next month, right here in the Elmwood Armory, Victor Koslov, I'm challenging you to a no holds barred, no disqualification, anything goes Legends Match! And Bruiser! Listen up! You better get ready, cuz right here next month it's gonna be you one on one against KOLE THE KRUSHER!"

As the show closed with Stan, Joey, and Kole raising their arms in solidarity, I remained at ringside, stunned by what I'd just witnessed. A magical angle had played out before me—complete with surprise returns, shocking betrayals, and emotional stakes— and I, the supposed right-hand man of the promotion, had been completely in the dark.

The more I thought about it, the clearer it became. I hadn't been kept out of the loop by accident—it had been deliberate. Stan had wanted my shock, my authentic confusion, visible at ringside. He'd made me part of the show without telling me.

I was pissed. And exhilarated.

FIFTY-FOUR

As the crowd filed out, I spotted Rachel making her way toward the back. She caught my eye and gave me a small, almost apologetic smile. Joey must have told her. Of course he did. He didn't want her to worry.

The ring crew was already moving—breaking down the barriers, coiling cables, restoring the Elmwood Armory to whatever it was the other six nights of the week. I watched them work for a minute before heading to the locker room.

Backstage, Victor was laughing with Stan as if there had never been any heat, and Kole was surrounded by well-wishers celebrating his surprise return.

"You should have seen your face," Joey said, appearing beside me. "You had no idea, did you?"

"Not a clue," I admitted.

Joey looked guilty. "Stan said to kayfabe you. That your reaction had to be real for it to work."

Fifteen years. After everything I'd done—every crisis I'd managed, every Friday night I'd chosen this over everything else—

when Stan needed something genuine, the most useful thing I had to offer was my own ignorance.

He wasn't wrong. It worked beautifully. The crowd felt it because I'd felt it. The shock on my face at ringside when Kole's music hit was real in a way that nothing planned could have been. Stan had known that. He understood people the way other men understood weather.

I wasn't angry. That was the strange part. But I wasn't quite sure what I was feeling.

Joey was watching me. "You okay?"

"Yeah," I said. "I'm good. Congrats on the engagement, by the way."

"How did you know?"

"I saw the ring on her finger. Good job."

"Thanks, Luke."

As the backstage celebration continued, Stan finally made his way over to me.

"So," he said, "what did you think?"

"I think you're a manipulative old carny who played me like a fiddle."

Stan's grin widened. "Is that a compliment or an insult?"

I looked at him the way you look at something when you've finally stopped hoping it'll turn into something else. The white hair, the solid frame, the once-handsome face. Sixty-three years old and he'd never once been off the clock. The business was the only thing he'd ever really loved. And he'd loved it by making everything serve it—the wrestlers, the money, the fans, the angles.

And me.

I'd handed in my notice at Silvertech and was ready to start my new role at Heartland—and my new life.

Maybe this was the right time to walk away from wrestling, too.

"So, Stan..." I started to say. And then I thought about what I would ask. I wanted to know what his plan was. And had the plan changed? And when did it change? And why was I always the one being kayfabed?

"Yeah, Luke?" Stan said.

"Good show," I squeaked out.

The room looked different once the ring was half-dismantled. The canvas was rolled up and waiting to be loaded into the truck. The ropes were stacked on the floor by the door.

It looked like exactly what it was—disassembled plywood and steel pipe and worn padding, a thing built and rebuilt a hundred different times and across dozens of years. That was the thing about this world that nobody who hadn't seen it could quite believe: how small it all got when you took it apart.

But I'd seen what it became when the lights went down and the music hit and the crowd was ready to believe. I'd watched men and women pour something real into a constructed thing and make it matter. I'd done it myself, in my way, clipboard in hand.

Stan had worked me. Not just tonight. He'd read me correctly and used it for his gain. That was who he was, and that wasn't going to change.

"Luke!" Stan's voice boomed from across the armory. He was standing with Chuck and one of the trainees, who undoubtedly had a question about who knows what. "Luke! I need you."

I'd been there for fifteen years of Fridays.

I couldn't imagine not being there for fifteen more.

Acknowledgments

This book wouldn't exist without the world that inspired it, and the people who let me be part of theirs.

To Roger, for making my dreams come true by giving me a role in the NWF. Everything I know about this business—the good, the broken, and the beautiful—is because of you.

To Chad, my favorite wrestler and the best Dad I know, for allowing me to be part of his journey. Watching you from the beginning of your career to making it to the big time—and being your friend throughout the journey—is the highest honor of my career.

To Jordan, for inspiring me to write this story in the first place.

To Brody, Brandon and Danielle, John F., John S., John D., Tony, Dustin, Stew, Star Wars Matt, Nate, Rick, Cyndi, Russ, Tim, Jesse, Josh, Chris H., Chris P., Rick, Greg, Jack, Christian, Adam, Luke, Noah D., Drake, Max, Jeremy, Nick, AJ, Austin, Nikki and Josh, Eddie, Nick and Liz, Ethan, Kris, Ryleigh, Theresa, Jimmy, Jim, Ollie, Shaun, Callie, Mike G., Garon, Carl, Brian, Noah B., Kellie, Amanda, Matt S., Sean, Sam, Dean, Cody, Jesse, Neil, Craig, Willie, Vegas, Tim and Tammy, and anyone I accidentally left out. To all of the men and women I've encountered in the NWF, the HWA, the MWA, and beyond—you gave me fifteen years of stories I couldn't make up if I tried. Some of you are in these pages. All of you are in the book's DNA.

To Tasia and Harrison, for reading early drafts and telling me what worked and what didn't.

And to the fans—the ones who show up to UAW halls and armories on Friday nights, who cheer for people they've never heard of, who believe in something they know isn't real because it *feels* real in the moments that matter. You are the reason any of this exists. Luke's journey is possible because of your love of what we do.

Thank you.

About the Author

Kirk Sheppard spent over twenty years in the world of independent professional wrestling, working as a producer, director, production coordinator, and in-ring talent for the Northern Wrestling Federation, one of the Midwest's longest-running independent promotions. During that time he helped build shows, develop talent, and shape the kind of experiences that *Rope Burn* attempts to capture—the chaos, the camaraderie, and the particular devotion of people who give everything to a world that runs on passion more than profit. In 2018, he was inducted into the NWF Hall of Fame.

He has also been a mental health counselor for over twenty years, now working in private practice. This career has given him a

different kind of ringside seat to the ways people love things that hurt them, stay in rooms that maybe they shouldn't, and find meaning in places the rest of the world doesn't always understand.
Rope Burn is his second novel, following *The Search Party.*

For more, go to kirksheppard.com.

 kirksheppard.substack.com
 instagram.com/kirk.sheppard.writer
facebook.com/kirksheppardwriter

ALSO BY KIRK SHEPPARD

Fiction

The Search Party

Stay - A Short Story

Non-Fiction

The Magic of It All

Broken Stools

Soul Audit

Jesus & Me